MARVEL
MONSTERS UNLEASHED!
WHEN TRULL ATTACKS!

W...
STEVE

D1018816

MARVEL
Los Angeles
New York

First Paperback Edition, October 2017
10 9 8 7 6 5 4 3 2 1
FAC-020093-17230
Printed in the United States of America

Designed by David Roe
Cover Illustration by Skan Srisuwan

Library of Congress Control Number: 2017931522
ISBN 978-1-368-00249-3

Visit marvelkids.com

SUSTAINABLE FORESTRY INITIATIVE Certified Sourcing
www.sfiprogram.org
SFI-00993

THIS LABEL APPLIES TO TEXT STOCK

"It all began . . . with the meteorite."
—H. P. Lovecraft, *The Colour Out of Space*

"Trull is totally without mercy! He won't care what he destroys in his conquest of Earth! We must warn the world before it's too late!"
—Stan Lee, *Tales to Astonish* #21

PROLOGUE

HAMMERS ~~ARE REALLY~~ useful tools. You can use them to smack nails into wood, remove nails, pound out dents, and about a hundred other things we're not thinking of right now. But there's something else hammers—rather, *a* hammer—can do: propel the person wielding it through the sky at remarkable speeds.

Try that with a hammer you buy at the hardware store and you're not going to get very far. But if you happened to be an Asgardian named Thor, and your hammer was an enchanted mallet called Mjolnir, then you'd be sitting pretty. Flying pretty. You know what we mean.

1

At that very moment, Thor found himself soaring through Earth's upper atmosphere. In his right hand he held fast to the leather strap that in turn was wrapped around Mjolnir's handle. In actuality, the hammer did the flying, and Thor held on for the ride. He had received a message from Nick Fury, the director of S.H.I.E.L.D., that something had gone wrong with one of their experimental aircrafts. The other Avengers were currently occupied, fighting against the Serpent Society somewhere in Antarctica. This left Thor as the lone Avenger available to help Fury and the Strategic Homeland Intervention Enforcement Logistics Division.

The Asgardian scanned the sky with the keenest of eyes. He had spotted the S.H.I.E.L.D. craft a minute before and was rapidly closing the gap between himself and the vehicle. It moved fast, Thor thought— faster than Iron Man, faster than an Avengers Quinjet. Thor continued to close the distance.

"Fury," Thor said into a miniaturized Avengers communicator. "I have your ship in view. It is fast, but not too fast for the son of Odin!"

Static crackled over the communicator, then Fury's voice. "Don't get too cocky, Thor. It's a drone, sure, but we're detecting that its weapons systems are fully armed and—"

Thor suppressed a chuckle. "At ease, Fury. I'm certain that I can handle anything your craft can—"

ZZZZRRRAAAAAAK!

Without warning, the craft fired a beam of ionic energy at Thor. The Asgardian reeled as his body surged with a paralyzing force. Ahead, the craft slowed abruptly and changed direction.

It was heading for Thor.

Momentarily caught off guard, Thor struggled in midair. Control over his muscles returned, and the Asgardian flung his mallet forward, propelling himself directly at the craft. "Have at thee!" he shouted. Mjolnir propelled him toward the ship, which fired pulses of ionic energy intended to take Thor down. Thor swooped left and right, up and down, avoiding every blast.

At last, he was upon the craft. He caught the wing with his left hand and swung in behind the ship. He looked inside the cockpit and saw no one. As Fury said, it was a drone. Computer-controlled. But if S.H.I.E.L.D. wasn't controlling the computer . . . who was?

Thor's mind immediately raced to the likely culprit. Ultron. The living robot had caused untold troubles for him and the other Avengers over the years. Could this be the opening of Ultron's latest scheme? Taking control of an experimental S.H.I.E.L.D. aircraft?

"Thor!" came Fury's voice over the communicator. "What's happening up there? We see the ship discharged its weapons. Are you okay?"

Before Thor could answer, the craft's hull began to surge with ionic energy. He let go of the wing just as the surge hit, flew backward, and caught the ship's tail.

"I am fine," Thor replied. "A bit busy. Is it possible Ultron has returned?"

"Negative," Fury said. "When we lost contact with the drone and saw that it was moving independently, that was the first thing we thought.

But Ultron is currently imprisoned—we have his consciousness trapped here on the Helicarrier in a single, non-networked computer. This is something else."

Something else, indeed, thought Thor. The rogue S.H.I.E.L.D. drone was now zigzagging through the sky, trying to shake Thor off its tail. Once again, the hero heard a humming come from within the craft—it was preparing another burst of ionic energy in an effort to dislodge Thor. Raising his right arm, Thor brought Mjolnir crashing into the hull of the ship. The hammer tore through metal as easily as a hand passes through water. What happened next surprised even the son of Odin.

Wires from inside the hole whipped with incredible force, lashing Thor's right hand to the hull of the ship. The wires were more like the tendrils of some wild beast of Asgardian legend. They moved with a mind of their own, attacking. Before Thor could react, more wires erupted from the surface of the craft, wrapping themselves around his legs and left arm. The wires pulled themselves taut, and now

Thor was held with his back against the hull of the ship.

He heard the humming once more. The ship was getting ready to fry him.

"What wickedness?" Thor exclaimed. How had a mere construct such as this ship overtaken him so swiftly, so surely? He didn't know, and he didn't care. But he decided this would end, and it would end now.

With all his might, Thor strained at the wires holding his right hand. Something else—some force—added strength to the wires, and it resisted him. But the hero would not relent. He managed to move his right hand up just enough so he could slam the blunt end of his hammer onto the hull.

The sky reacted with the fury of the storm.

Thunder.

Rain.

And lightning.

Lightning, which struck from the heavens above, dancing all over the rogue S.H.I.E.L.D. craft. At once, the wires that held Thor prisoner let go. The ship's circuits were overloaded with more raw energy than it could possibly handle. Thor flung himself from the craft, flying alongside it now. As Thor watched the craft, he saw it do the impossible. It stopped in midair while the lightning continued to strike it. The craft moved down, then up. Then it tried to move backward.

It was as if it had a mind of its own.

The lightning continued until the ship blew itself into a million pieces.

Thor called off the storm. As he did, he noticed something peculiar. He saw a yellow cloud of some kind streaming from the explosion, slowly drifting upward toward space. . . .

◦ ◦ ◦

Midnight.

A brilliant ball of light streaked across the sky of a nameless Northeastern town.

A meteor.

The object hurtled toward the ground for the inevitable impact. In the middle of nowhere, in the middle of the night, there was no one around to

observe its explosive arrival. The meteor slammed into solid rock and slid for at least a hundred yards before coming to a halt.

It landed inside an old quarry filled with abandoned crushing and drilling equipment. There was an old dump truck there as well, upended by the meteor's crash.

And then a curious thing happened. The abandoned equipment hummed to life.

So did the old dump truck, which righted itself, then drove off into the night.

CHAPTER

1

"THIS SUCKS!" a voice shouted.

The voice belonged to ten-year-old Louisa Brooks. So did the attitude.

"Louisa . . ." said her mom, hoping to cut her daughter off from launching into the same exact speech she had been listening to ever since their family announced they were moving to the small town of Woodstock.

Her hope didn't last long.

"Mom, it's totally unfair!" Louisa began. "It's summer! As in summer vacation? I should be hanging out with my friends, having the time of my life! But what am I doing instead?"

"By 'friends,' I assume you mean 'books,'" said her dad, removing the glasses from his face. Mr. Brooks rubbed his eyes, tired from the long drive to the family's new home. He looked at his daughter, then cracked a smile.

Louisa smiled back in spite of herself.

"Books, friends, same thing!" Louisa replied, using a hand to shield her eyes from the afternoon sun. "All I know is, I was looking forward to having the whole summer to sit in the library and read, and *now* look! Here we are, in the middle of nowhere. I bet there isn't a decent library around here for miles!"

Louisa looked at her feet and kicked the dirt outside her new home. An avid reader, Louisa was well on her way to building an impressive library of her own. But nothing could replace her love for an actual public library. During the summer, she practically lived in the library in her old town. She was there almost every day, devouring book after book. Fiction, nonfiction, it didn't matter. There were fairy tales, biographies, books about Super Heroes (her favorite was the Wasp), graphic novels, and more. There wasn't a subject that Louisa didn't find fascinating.

"Louisa!" snapped her mother, trying to get her daughter's attention. "You drifted off again, honey. Come on back to us!" She gave a little laugh, and Louisa couldn't help but to laugh right back. "I swear, you do so much living inside your head. I'd love to know what's going on in there! Let's go in the house. Maybe seeing your room would help take your mind off of things. Now, help me with these boxes."

Louisa shrugged her shoulders and made a face that said, *I guess so.* She picked up a box of her stuff and walked into the house.

It was an older house, two floors. She had a big bedroom of her own on the second floor. There was plenty of room for her ever-growing collection of books.

Once inside, Louisa thought the place looked a little older than it did on the outside. And it was all kinds of creaky. Definitely creaky. As Louisa walked up the stairs to her room, each individual step let out a soft moan beneath her feet. There was something about the old wood that she decided she liked.

Her room was right at the top of the stairs, opposite a small bathroom. Her own bathroom. That was pretty cool. The room wasn't bad, either. It was actually pretty huge. It ran the length of the house. Half of the ceiling was a massive skylight. Sunlight poured into the room. There were several nooks and crannies, perfect for storage. Best of all were the built-in bookshelves that lined a whole wall of her room. She couldn't believe it. Louisa wouldn't admit it to her parents, but the bookshelves alone might have made the move worthwhile.

The kitchen was unpacked. Kind of. Sort of. Enough so that the family could make a meal, or at least eat the meal they had ordered from the local pizzeria. Two large pepperoni-and-pineapple pizzas sat on the table in front of Louisa and her parents. The first pizza was almost entirely devoured, and Louisa had her heart set on at least a couple of slices from the second one.

"I don't know about you two," Mrs. Brooks said as she took a bite of pepperoni, "but I am beat! This has been a really long day."

Louisa nodded. "I know, my arms are killing me! And I still have all my books to put away!"

Mr. Brooks nibbled at the crust of a pizza slice. "You don't have to get it all done today," he said, munching away. "You know, we're probably going to be living here more than one day."

Louisa laughed. "I know, but I just want to get settled in. I want to go to bed tonight knowing that all my books are right at my fingertips so when I wake up in the morning, I can dive right in."

Mrs. Brooks finished the slice she was eating and stood up from the table. "Once you have your mind set on something, it stays set," she said, running her hand through Louisa's hair.

Louisa looked at her mom, uncertain. Her mom laughed.

"That's a good thing, honey," Mrs. Brooks said, and Louisa sighed in relief. "It means you feel strongly about things. And speaking of feeling strongly about things, I feel strongly that I need to get some sleep. We have an early start tomorrow at Win-X."

Mr. Brooks finished eating his crust, then got up from the table, too. "I think I'll join you. Louisa, will you put the leftover pizza in the fridge so Ash doesn't have himself a midnight snack?"

"You bet, Dad," Louisa said. Her parents left the kitchen, as Louisa quickly finished her pizza.

The books were waiting.

Louisa tiptoed up the stairs to her room. Once inside, she quietly shut the door and took a good look. The movers had brought her bed and desk inside, along with most of her things. There was only one thing left for Louisa to do. She worked like crazy, unpacking box after box of books.

While her parents were downstairs, getting a good night's sleep before their first day at the power plant, Louisa remained holed up in her new room. One by one, the shelves were filled up. By the time she unpacked the last box, it was after midnight. Louisa climbed into her bed and admired her handy work. The wall was covered in rows and rows of colorful book spines. She then reached over, pulled the cord on her bedside lamp, and promptly fell asleep.

CHAPTER 2

LOUISA LOVED the idea of having a big skylight in her bedroom. The skylight meant lots and lots of sun. Unfortunately, that also meant lots and lots of sun first thing in the morning, when all she wanted to do was sleep in.

The rude sun burned through her eyelids and woke Louisa up on her very first full day in the new house.

She yawned and stretched, and rubbed her eyes with both hands. Then she yawned some more, and heard a loud creaking.

"Wait, is that me?" she said out loud. Was that her bones creaking? No, it wasn't her bones! She

sat in her bed, waiting for the sound to come once more.

CREEEEAAAAAAK!

There it was again. It seemed to be coming from somewhere downstairs. A second later, Louisa heard barking coming from the same direction. The bark belonged to Ash, her four-legged best friend.

"Ash? Come on up, buddy!" Louisa called out. Usually the dog would come running whenever he heard his name. But not today. Instead, the bark quickly became a whimper.

Then nothing.

"Ash?" Louisa asked. "Mom? Dad?" she called out, then waited.

No one said anything back.

Louisa was getting a weird, creepy vibe. Like the kind of vibe she got when she stayed up too late reading the complete works of Edgar Allan Poe. Poe was her dad's favorite author, and he delighted in reading the scary stories and spooky poems to Louisa.

CREEEEEEEAAAAAAAAAK!

There came the creaking noise from downstairs, again. Followed by a . . . a buzzing of some kind. Like static? It sounded like something electric.

Sliding the covers off her legs, Louisa quietly planted her feet on the bare hardwood and walked slowly toward her bedroom door. The floor squeaked gently beneath her feet.

"*While I nodded, nearly napping, suddenly there came a tapping . . .*" she said to herself. "The Raven" was one of her favorite poems by Poe. For like a year straight, Louisa had asked her dad to read it to her at bedtime. Now, when she was really nervous or afraid, Louisa would sometimes recite the poem to herself. It helped her to calm down and get a handle on her fear.

Opening the door, Louisa stepped into the hallway and looked down the stairs. There was nothing out of place, nothing out of the ordinary.

CREEEEEEAAAAAAAKKK!

Louisa jumped back at the sound. The creak wasn't coming from the stairs. It was coming from somewhere else. Again, she heard the sound of static. It filled her ears now as it grew louder and louder.

Step by step, Louisa crept down the flight of stairs. *"As of some one gently rapping, rapping at my chamber door . . ."* she said softly. *" 'Tis some visitor,' I muttered, 'tapping at my chamber door—Only this and nothing more.'"*

She really hoped it was "nothing more" than an old house and her overactive imagination. Maybe her dad shouldn't have been reading all those Edgar Allan Poe stories to her when she was so young, she thought.

Once at the bottom of the stairs, Louisa looked around. The moving boxes were still there, untouched from last night. Everything was quiet and there was a stillness in the air. She didn't hear any of the usual morning activity—not her parents making breakfast, nor her dog. There was only the static, which came from the kitchen. It was growing louder and louder.

"Deep into that darkness peering, long I stood there wondering, fearing . . ." Louisa muttered, creeping

toward the kitchen. Why was she so on edge? Her parents were probably hiding, waiting to surprise her in their new home.

But what about Ash? Maybe they had taken him outside for a long walk? That must be it.

The static grew louder in her ears.

"Doubting, dreaming dreams no mortal ever dared to dream before . . ."

Louisa turned the corner and looked inside the kitchen.

There were her parents.

And Ash.

They were screaming.

But no sound escaped their mouths.

The static grew louder as Louisa ran to help them, but the more she ran, the farther away from her family she became. She ran harder and faster, and yet the distance between her and her parents only grew. What was going on?

Her family was reaching for her, still screaming silently. Louisa watched in horror as extension cords from all over the house snaked into the kitchen and began wrapping themselves around her mom, her dad, and Ash.

The static grew so loud, Louisa thought her head would explode.

She screamed.

No sound came out.

CHAPTER 3

"AHHHHHHHHHHHHHHHHHHH!!!!"

Louisa shot bolt upright in bed. Sun poured through the skylight, and sweat poured off her forehead. She looked around her room, to the left and to the right. She saw her desk, some moving boxes, and her books. The books were right where she had put them last night.

"It was just a dream, it was just a dream," she said to herself, over and over. She looked around her room, breathing heavily. Louisa tried to quiet herself so she could hear sound coming from the rest of her house.

Then she heard them. Her mom and dad. In the kitchen.

Talking.

Louisa let out a sigh and said, *"Let my heart be still a moment . . . 'Tis the wind and nothing more!"*

What was that nightmare all about? she wondered. Louisa wasn't used to having nightmares, and certainly not one that was so full of dread. It left her feeling a little dizzy, and afraid. She put her head back down on her pillow, burying her face in it. Maybe she could squeeze out a few more minutes of sleep, she thought. Something to help erase the memory of that wild dream. Her eyelids felt heavy, and she could feel herself starting to drift. . . .

"Louisa? Are you awake, honey?" her mom called from the bottom of the stairs.

Louisa let out a big sigh. She wanted to go back to sleep, but that wasn't going to happen now.

"Yeah . . . Be down in a minute!" Louisa yelled.

◦ ◦ ◦

Despite the creepy nightmare, Louisa was in a slightly better mood than she had been in yesterday. The first night in the new home was officially under her belt. Louisa was not the kind of girl to let a bad dream ruin her day.

Louisa rubbed her eyes, let out one final yawn, and walked over to her dresser. When she opened the top drawer, she jumped, startled. It was completely empty! It took her a second but then she put her palm over her face.

Wow, really, Louisa? she thought. She had forgotten that she didn't put any of her clothes in the empty dresser last night. She was way too focused on her books and had fallen asleep before she could put on her pajamas. All of her clothes were all still neatly packed away in moving boxes. *I guess I'm still a little frazzled,* she thought. From the nightmare or moving to a new place, she couldn't tell.

Louisa walked over to one of her larger moving boxes marked LOUISA'S CLOTHES in her mom's careful handwriting. She pried back the cardboard and pulled out the first thing she saw. It was her favorite white blouse with a Peter Pan collar. She loved the way the white popped against her dark complexion and how the collar made her feel like Fern from *Charlotte's Web*. All she needed was her pet pig. That's probably why her parents got her Ash. Also because dogs tend to be much cleaner than pigs.

Louisa reached into the box again and pulled out a burgundy sweater and black jeans. Even though it was early summer, the air still had a slight chill to it. After she quickly dressed herself and brushed out the tangles in her long hair, Louisa walked over to her newly organized collection of books. Scanning the shelves, she decided that she was in an Avengers frame of mind. She picked out a book of photographs taken by *Daily Bugle* photographer Phil Sheldon called *Marvels*. Inside were amazing pictures of the Avengers in action, along with a host of other Super Heroes. On the front cover was an amazing photo of the towering Giant-Man. Her mom and dad had given it to her as a moving present, and she couldn't wait to dig in.

The creaking stairs announced Louisa as she

bounded down, two steps at a time. She hit the floor at the bottom of the stairs with both feet, hard. Unlike her old home, there were no downstairs neighbors here, and Louisa could make as much noise as she wanted. Even still, she was counting down the seconds inside her head until she heard her mother say . . .

"Louisa! No heavy feet!" her mom scolded from the kitchen.

Well, almost as much noise as she wanted.

Inside the kitchen, Louisa's mom was busy making sandwiches for her and Mr. Brooks. Mr. Brooks was at the stove, making scrambled eggs and bacon. Watching all this food-related activity with keen interest was Louisa's dog, Ash. Half Labrador retriever and half goofball, Ash had been Louisa's companion since she was four. The grayish-black dog raced back and forth between Louisa's mom and dad, hoping, begging for a free meal that never came.

"Eggs?" Mr. Brooks said, and Louisa nodded.

"Yes, they are," Louisa replied, earning a broad

smile from her dad. "So, you guys are really going to work, huh?"

Louisa sat down at the table. She set the book down right next to her. Ash ran over to Louisa, checking to see if she had any food. She didn't, so he settled for a few friendly pats on his head. "You going to work too, Ash?"

"Just for a half day today," said Mr. Brooks as he served Louisa a plate of bacon and eggs. "Me, I mean. And your mom. Ash isn't going to work. He's still looking for a job," he joked. Then he set down a bottle of ketchup next to her. He knew Louisa well. "It'll be longer hours starting tomorrow. But the plant is almost up and running. They need us."

"The plant" was officially known as Win-X. It was a wind farm—a plant with hundreds of wind turbines that generated cheap, renewable electricity. That was the reason why Louisa had moved to Woodstock in the first place. Her parents had been instrumental in the creation of Win-X. And now that it was close to opening, the company had asked Mr.

and Mrs. Brooks to help manage the power plant.

Louisa took a bite of her eggs. Her dad's eggs were the best—a dash of pepper, a little hot sauce, and a few drops of milk gave them a kick that she loved. Then that squeeze of ketchup made them perfect. Of course, what Louisa thought was a "squeeze" was what her parents called "half the bottle." She looked up from her plate as her parents finished getting ready for work.

"When you're done eating, remember to clean your dishes," her mom said. "And don't put them on the floor so Ash can 'clean' them, either! Then you can head out on your bike. Maybe explore the neighborhood . . . make some new friends . . ."

Louisa frowned. Making friends didn't come easy to her. Her parents were her friends. Books were her friends. Still, she knew that getting outside the house wasn't a bad idea. She could always bring a book with her. And who knew? Maybe she might find the public library . . . if this tiny town even had one.

CHAPTER

4

WITH HER PARENTS long gone, Louisa watched as Ash ran around the kitchen sniffing for any scraps of food that might have fallen on the floor. There were none. He gave one last hopeful glance at Louisa. Disappointed, the dog ran out of the kitchen.

"Don't worry, I'll clean up," Louisa yelled out to Ash. "I appreciate your offer to help, really! But I got this. You just go do . . . dog stuff."

Louisa got up from the table and took her plate to the sink, washed it, and set it in the drying rack. From the living room, she heard Ash's paws on the hardwood floor, his nails click-clicking along.

She made herself a to-go bag with an apple and a string cheese stick, and took it with her as she left the kitchen and headed through the living room on the way to the garage. She saw Ash sitting on the couch, which was behind several rows of opened moving boxes. The dog poked his head up to watch Louisa walk by, then put it back down on the couch with a soft grumble.

"No, don't get up," Louisa kidded Ash. "See ya later, buddy. She opened the door to the garage. Waiting inside was her bike and helmet. She strapped the helmet on and walked her bike out to the driveway. Then she pressed the button next to the garage and closed the large door. She hopped on her bike, then rode out into the street.

It was time to finally get out and explore this town.

Louisa had circled her neighborhood three or four times before giving up. She didn't see any signs of kids outside, playing or doing anything else, for that matter. What did she expect? That there would be a big group of approachable, friendly kids playing near her house? Louisa sighed. The little town was making a very bad first impression. Or maybe she wasn't giving it enough of a chance. Either way, Louisa was bored.

She thought about the book she started reading that morning, *Marvels*. Louisa felt a little like Phil Sheldon—a kind of quiet person who kept to himself, but who liked to be around the action. To really see things. Not just read about them, but to experience them. What would it be like to watch Spider-Man tackle Doctor Octopus on top of a New York City skyscraper? Or to see Iron Man and his incredible armor up close? Or to hang out on a rooftop while Ms. Marvel took out that weird half-human, half-bird hybrid, the Inventor? Those things seemed very far away from the world in which Louisa lived.

"Well, I can keep moping around my neighborhood, or try to find *something* to do," said Louisa. A part of her really wanted to mope, and thought about doing that for the rest of the day. But then she decided to make the best of things. She pushed on the ground with her left foot, sending the bicycle forward.

It was midday and Louisa's eyes were beginning to feel heavy. Her first night in her new house wasn't exactly the best sleep she'd ever had. The nightmare she had stuck in her mind, and she couldn't seem to shake it.

That was when she saw it.

A library.

An actual, honest-to-goodness public library. In her town, no less! Louisa figured it was about a half-hour bike ride from her house, give or take a few minutes. She didn't even realize that she had been trying to find it all day. It almost felt like a mirage—you know, like those lakes people see in the desert when they're dying of thirst? But it wasn't a mirage. It was one of the best places on earth.

Louisa pedaled down the street to the red-and-brown brick building. There was only one car in the parking lot, and there was a bicycle rack right near the front door. Louisa stopped next to the rack, hopped off, and slid her bike between the metal bars. She didn't bother locking it—after all, there was no one around to steal anything in this town.

She pulled the front door open and walked inside. She was home.

THE OLD DUMP TRUCK rumbled down the road, kicking up a cloud of dirt and dust as it sped along. It had been on the road since last night. The "empty" light was on inside the cab—the truck had been driving on fumes for the last mile or so, and it slowly came to a halt on the side of the road. There was wide-open space on either side of the road. Corn fields were on the left. Soybean plants were on the right. There was no sound other than a few crows cawing in the distance.

The truck sat there, motionless.

There was no driver inside the cab.

Or anywhere else around the truck, for that matter.

Because the truck never had a driver.

Not a human one.

The truck's headlights flickered on and off for a moment. Then the radio came on. It started on the left of the dial, then quickly moved from station to station, all the way to the top. Along the way, a small, tinny sound came out of the speakers:

"Trulltrulltrulltrulltrulltrulltrulltrull . . ."

Then, as quickly as it came on, the radio turned off.

There was silence.

From the opposite direction, a red pickup truck was traveling down the highway. The bed of the truck was filled with old televisions, toasters, radios—appliances that no longer worked and that no one wanted. On the side of the truck were the words WURTZER'S SALVAGE.

The driver was an older woman, and she wore

thick glasses and a bright blue baseball cap. As she moved down the highway, she saw a truck up in the distance, pulled over on the side of the road.

Probably someone'll be needing a lift, she thought. She pulled over, then got out of her pickup. The woman was wearing jean overalls, and she pushed the baseball cap back on her head.

"Hello!" she called out on the deserted road. "Need help? Looks like your truck died. I expect you want a lift." She paused. "Well, I'm heading out to the next town over to drop off this junk. You're welcome to tag along."

There was no answer.

The woman took off her cap, scratched her head, and put it back on. She walked across the road and over to the dump truck. She didn't see anybody when she looked inside the cab.

"Hello?" she said again. Her answer was silence.

If the woman was being honest, this situation was creepy.

Who would just leave a truck out here in the middle of nowhere? the woman thought. She walked around the dump truck, and listened to the sound of gravel crunching under her work boots. Something about the truck seemed familiar. Then it came to her.

The abandoned rock quarry. This was one of the old dump trucks they would use to haul away the massive boulders! She knew because she used to work in the quarry as a driller. But the quarry closed down four years ago when the company went bankrupt. Overnight, the owners abandoned the site, leaving all the equipment there to rust. So how did the dump truck get out here? Maybe kids playing a prank?

RRRRRRRRRRRRRRRRRRRRRRRRR!

Without warning, the dump truck revved its engine, which quickly sputtered. The sudden sound made the woman jump away from the truck and scream.

"What the devil . . . ?"

The truck started to shudder and shake. Then a fine, yellow mist seemed to seep out from the vehicle, forming a cloud that hovered right above it. The woman stared, slack jawed, unable to move.

The yellow cloud began to drift. Toward the red pickup truck.

A moment later, the cloud entered the pickup truck through its tailpipe. The woman watched with her mouth open as the pickup truck roared to life, its engine screaming. Then it accelerated, making a half circle and nearly hitting the woman, who managed to dive out of the way.

The red pickup truck with no driver rolled down the road, heading who knew where.

CHAPTER 6

"THIS IS THE BEST PLACE EVER!"
Louisa cried out, before remembering that she was in a public library and crying out was absolutely the last thing you should do.

She totally expected to hear a loud "shush" come from the librarian, but she didn't. In fact, she realized she hadn't even seen a librarian since she'd entered the library twenty minutes before. She hadn't seen anyone, in fact. Louisa had the library all to herself.

The library was truly impressive, especially for such a small town. The place was packed from floor to ceiling with books, including an incredible selection of new titles. And based on Louisa's quick reading of the library's policies, what she didn't see on the shelves could be ordered from a network of other libraries and delivered right here.

To a hungry reader like Louisa, it was heaven.

"A hungry reader" was right—she had been so caught up in the joy of exploring the library, she had forgotten that not only was she exhausted but also her stomach was screaming for food. She had her snack bag inside her backpack, and she resolved to polish it off as soon as she finished up at the library.

"I don't know about the 'best place ever,' but it's pretty good," came a voice from behind a big stack of books on the counter.

Louisa turned her head from a book about the Apollo space program, and looked over to the front desk. There was a woman, maybe five feet tall, with glasses and pink hair.

A librarian with pink hair? Now that was cool, Louisa thought.

"I'm sorry for being so loud," Louisa babbled. "I didn't mean to disturb anybody. I love libraries and

I'm always so quiet, I promise, and please don't kick me out and—"

By now the woman could hardly contain herself, and was laughing uncontrollably. She held up a hand as if to reassure Louisa that everything was going to be just fine. "You're okay," the librarian said, still chuckling. "We're the only two people here, and I'm happy to have the company of another book lover. My name is Ms. Pratt. Who are you?"

Louisa sighed, happy to not be in trouble. "I'm Louisa. Louisa Brooks. We just moved here, and I thought there wasn't going to be anything good to do, but then I found this library, and wow!"

"I'm glad you like it!" Ms. Pratt said as she picked a few books up off the stack and walked them over to a nearby cart. She put the books down, then walked over to Louisa, her right hand extended. Louisa stared at the woman for a moment, before realizing they were supposed to shake hands. Louisa awkwardly put our her right hand, and they shook.

"Pleased to meet you, Louisa. Anything you're looking for today?"

Louisa took a deep breath. She could practically smell all the books. Then she smiled at Ms. Pratt. "I've been reading *Marvels*," she said. "Do you have anything else like it?"

"*Marvels* . . ." said Ms. Pratt, her voice trailing off in thought. "By Phil Sheldon?"

Louisa nodded.

"That's a great book! Such amazing photos. His photograph of Giant-Man walking over the streets of New York City is really incredible. You know, you might like a book called *Webs*. It's also by a *Daily Bugle* photographer. Peter Parker. It's nothing but wall-to-wall pictures of Spider-Man in action."

Louisa's eyes lit up. "That sounds perfect!" She had heard of the book, and certainly knew who Peter Parker was. But the book had only come out as a limited print run and was super-expensive—if you could even find a copy in a used bookstore. Louisa thought she'd never get to read it.

"All right, then! It's 'photography,' so that would be . . ."

Before Ms. Pratt could finish, Louisa jumped right

in. "Would it be in the 770s, with Photography? Or is it in the 900s, for History? Or maybe it's—"

Ms. Pratt stared at Louisa and raised her right eyebrow over the rim of her glasses. "Are you trying to tell me that you have the Dewey Decimal System memorized?"

Louisa blushed.

"Anybody who knows the Dewey Decimal System is a friend of mine for life," Ms. Pratt said.

There was a loud gurgling sound.

Louisa's stomach.

She blushed again.

"You sound pretty hungry," Ms. Pratt said, laughing. "Did you bring food with you? You can go ahead and eat it, if you want. I won't tell."

Louisa smiled. She really was home.

CHAPTER 7

KEI WAS ~~BEAT.~~ Beyond tired. He just wanted to sleep. He could feel his eyes drooping, and the pencil he held in his right hand felt like it weighed a ton.

Things had been super-busy lately. Sure, school was out for the summer, so he didn't have the typical homework and activities and everything else that went along with it. He had hoped that he'd have a couple of months to kick back, relax, and do what he loved the most—create monsters.

But stuff has a way of happening when you least expect it, and that was exactly how it was with Kei. One minute, he was minding his own business. The next—WHAM! Up pops a creepy creature called the Glop, and he's sending Slizzik to help a couple of kids destroy it. Or he was sitting in his room, drawing, then—BAM! Racing around trying to save a good-hearted Gorgilla from a group of sinister scientists. Not to mention all the stuff that had been going on with the Avengers, and more monsters than Kei could count.

Well, that wasn't exactly true. He could definitely count them all. That was kind of his hobby, after all. Cataloging and keeping track of monsters on talestoastonish.com. He liked doing that. He liked helping people almost as much as he enjoyed drawing and creating new monsters in his sketchbook.

He was sitting at his desk in his bedroom, and he ran a hand through his thick, shaggy black hair. Then he yawned. He stared at the blank piece of paper in front of him. His eyes closed for a second, then Kei startled, his eyes blinking.

"Huh? Who?" Kei said to no one. He realized he had almost fallen asleep sitting up in his chair!

While he wanted nothing more than to shuffle

over to his bed and go back to sleep, Kei knew he couldn't. If he fell asleep in the middle of the day, his mom would come home later, find him in bed, and then she'd be on him. "You're wasting the summer away!" she'd say. "You should be outside, having fun! Not cooped up in your room, drawing in your books all day long!"

Ugh. Moms.

Kei picked up the pencil from the desk, and sharpened it to a fine point. Then he poked himself in the arm. "Gotta stay awake," he said. He rubbed the little gray spot on his arm.

Blinking the sleep out of his eyes, Kei started to move the pencil along the blank page. What would he draw today? What kind of creature would he conjure? He had designed some really cool ones lately. They had helped out in some pretty big battles against some pretty tough foes the last couple of months.

That was because Kei wasn't just an average, ordinary kid. Sometimes he went by another name. Kid Kaiju. The monster kid. Because Kei had super powers—whatever he drew on the page could come to life.

Pretty cool, huh?

Right now, Kei was racking his tired brain, trying to come up with a totally different kind of monster. Something he had never come up with before. He kept moving the pencil, sketching, then looked at the paper.

He had drawn a lightbulb inside a big circle. Then he had drawn a line through the circle, across the lightbulb.

"I have no ideas," he said, and his head fell down on his desk. "What am I going to do?"

Kei picked his head up off the desk, then leaned back in his chair. He took a long, deep breath. He grabbed his phone and started to swipe through his apps. For a split second, Kei thought about going outside and catching some dumplings in his new favorite game, *Pork Bun Go*, but he was feeling pretty lazy at the moment. Messages, *Tales to Astonish*, Weather, News. Kei paused for a moment, his thumb hovering over his news app. Maybe the Avengers were off fighting somewhere and needed his help. He opened the app and began to scroll. He stopped when he saw a headline that read:

MASSIVE POWER OUTAGE
CAUSES SMALL TOWN TO SHUT DOWN

Kei stared at the screen, then at his paper, and then at the lightbulb.

And he had an actual idea.

"No . . . you're kidding me!" Kei said, leaning forward in his chair. A smile appeared on his face, and he flipped the page in the sketchbook to a blank piece of paper. "A lightbulb! That's it!"

Pencil in hand, Kei began sketching anew.

He roughed in a large, hulking figure. This monster would be a big guy, and look like a fighter—a bruiser. Kei started to give him little spikes on his back and arms, too. But he wasn't just a big, bulky monster. No, the lightbulb had given Kei the idea—this monster would be made of electricity!

After a while, Kei put his pencil down and took

a look at his handiwork. He smiled. Staring back at him was a bluish-white creature with bright white electric eyes, and a zigzagging white line for a mouth. It looked like the creature was smiling, too.

"You need a name," Kei said to himself. "Let's see . . . electricity . . . watts . . . high voltage . . ." His voice trailed off.

"You look like a Hi-Vo," he said.

CHAPTER 8

"**WHERE ~~ARE YOU~~** heading off to so early?" Louisa's mom said. While her parents made lunch and got ready for work, Louisa had made herself some toast with peanut butter and banana, wrapped it in waxed paper, and put it in a bag.

"The library, duh," she said. "Where else?"

Mrs. Brooks smiled and shook her head. "Of course, what was I thinking? Where else would you be going at eight in the morning?"

Mr. Brooks looked up from the sandwich he was making. "The library opens up this early?" he said, skeptically.

Louisa shoved her meal into her backpack and picked up the copy of *Webs* that she had taken out from the library last week. "No, but Ms. Pratt gets in early, and she'll let me in."

"Who's Ms. Pratt, again?" her dad asked. He had that look on his face that said, *I know, you already told me, and I'm sorry I don't remember the answer.*

Louisa rolled her eyes, then grinned at her dad—he was forgiven. "She's the librarian, remember? You've asked me, like, ten times already. She's supercool and she has pink hair and she knows all sorts of cool books."

"Sounds like a good friend," Mrs. Brooks said. "I'd love to meet her sometime. Maybe we could all go to the library this weekend!"

The thought hadn't occurred to Louisa, but her mom was right. Ms. Pratt was more than just a librarian. In a very short time, she had become one of Louisa's best friends. Her only friend in this new town, certainly. It was a comforting thought.

"Yeah, totally," Louisa said, smiling. "Well, I'm off! Say 'hey' to the wind for me!" She gave her mom a big hug, turned around, and hugged her dad, too. Ash came trotting through the kitchen and ran right up to Louisa, his tail swiping against her leg. She gave him a pat on the head, then left through the garage, slamming the door behind her.

"For someone who likes quiet and reading books, she sure knows how to make a racket," Mr. Brooks said, laughing.

It was a hot summer day, probably the hottest so far. The outside temperature had to be near one hundred degrees. Luckily, Louisa was nestled inside the public library, all comfy and cozy in the air-conditioned environment. She had returned the copy of *Webs* to Ms. Pratt and was already looking for something else Super Hero–related to read. She had found a really neat book called *From Asgard to Zarrko: Thor A to Z*. While she considered herself something of a Spider-Man expert, Louisa didn't know nearly as much about Thor. This book seemed like a great place to start.

"I wonder who Zarrko is, anyway," Louisa said to

herself quietly as she flipped through the pages of the book.

"The Tomorrow Man," Ms. Pratt said from behind her desktop computer.

"Who the what, now?" said Louisa, making Ms. Pratt laugh. "What's a Tomorrow Man?"

"Artur Zarrko. You're talking about the guy who fought Thor? He came from the twenty-third century, or something like that. He tried to steal a bunch of weapons from our time and bring them back so he could conquer his own time."

"That doesn't sound like a plan that would work," Louisa observed.

Ms. Pratt laughed. "You're right. It didn't work. Thor saw to that. Read the book, it's a good one! Everything you ever wanted to know about Thor, Asgard, and in between."

The fluorescent lights above flickered for a moment, then came back on. Louisa kept flipping through the book, looking at pictures of some of the most powerful Asgardian warriors, like Sif. Again, the lights flickered.

"Ugh, the lights in this place are driving me nuts," said Ms. Pratt. "And I just had the bulbs replaced last month. Let me see if turning them off and then back on h—"

A fluorescent bulb exploded, raining broken glass.

"Oh!" shouted Ms. Pratt, and Louisa looked up, startled at the sound.

Then another fluorescent bulb shattered.

Then another.

And then the lights went out entirely, along with all the power in the library.

CHAPTER 9

"THIS HAPPENS all the time, right?" Louisa said. "Exploding lights? The power going out? Just a small-town kinda thing?" She bit her lip nervously.

"Nope," Ms. Pratt replied. "Not all the time. Second time. Weird. It's sunny and beautiful out. I could understand if there was a storm that knocked out the power, but this is just weird."

Louisa thought about what Ms. Pratt said. "Second time? What was the first time?"

Ms. Pratt got up from behind the computer and walked over to Louisa. The air-conditioning had been off for only a couple of minutes, but it was already growing warmer inside the library. "The first time was a couple of days ago, the night the comet appeared in the sky."

That got Louisa's attention but quick. "Comet? What comet? There was a comet? Here?" Her words poured out of her mouth faster than her lips could work. Louisa's mind was already running away from her with wild ideas.

"Not right here in the library. I mean, there wouldn't be a library left if a comet hit this place," Ms. Pratt said, joking. Louisa stared at Ms. Pratt wide-eyed, unblinking, nodding. "Boy, you're really serious about this comet, aren't you?"

"Ms. Pratt, it's something actually exciting! I thought this summer was going to just be spent reading books in here—no offense, you know I love books—but an actual comet? Tell me all about it!"

Ms. Pratt sat down next to Louisa. "There isn't too much to tell," she began. "The newspaper said a comet was reportedly seen streaking over the sky. There was some rumor that it hit near the old rock quarry way out by the interstate, but other than some old rusty machines and a big hole, they didn't find much of anything. Sorry to say it isn't more exciting than that."

"What do you mean, it isn't exciting? It's amazing!" Louisa gasped. "It's like *The War of the Worlds*! You know, the Martians coming down to our planet like meteors."

"An H. G. Wells fan?" Ms. Pratt asked.

Louisa nodded. "Well, yeah! He practically invented science fiction. Not like Jules Verne. I mean, that guy wrote some good stories, but it's not like flying around the world in a balloon is science fiction."

Ms. Pratt smiled, not saying anything in response.

"I was babbling, wasn't I?" Louisa said. Then, getting back to the matter at hand, Louisa asked, "Do you think the comet has something to do with the power going out?"

"I'm not sure," Ms. Pratt said. "I suppose it's possible. Maybe some kind of atmospheric disturbance? Something to do with static electricity?"

"Really?" Louisa shot back.

Ms. Pratt laughed. "I'm just guessing, kiddo! I'm not a scientist—"

"Yes, you are!"

"A *library* scientist. Not the same thing!"

The temperature in the library slowly climbed upward, and Louisa wiped her brow with the back of her hand.

"It's getting hot in here. Why don't you take your *Thor A to Z* home, and we'll pick up our discussion tomorrow? I can't wait for you to find out all about the Stone Men from Saturn."

"Stone Men from . . ." Louisa said, her voice trailing off. "Wait, that's a thing?"

It was hot. Really hot. Like, lava hot. Louisa pedaled her bike away from the library, wishing that she was old enough to drive a car. She loved being outside, but there was such a thing as too much heat. Oh, well. At least she could head home and read her Thor book from the comfort of her own air-conditioned bedroom.

As she pedaled through the neighborhood on her way back home, Louisa noticed that the power wasn't just off at the library. When she rode through the small downtown street, she saw the few stores there were without power.

"Weird," she said. "Did the comet do this, too?"

She kept on riding and passed by a house that was under construction. There was a big backhoe, the kind used to dig foundations for buildings. There were three burly construction workers standing next to it with their hard hats off. They inspected the backhoe, scratching their heads. Louisa stopped her bike.

". . . darnedest thing I ever saw," said one of the construction workers. Louisa missed the first part of what they were saying, but knew what they were talking about.

"How does a backhoe just lose power?" asked another construction worker. "It's not like it's plugged into anything!"

The construction workers were so focused on the backhoe that they didn't notice Louisa. She started pedaling and headed for home.

How can all the power be off? she thought. *For everything?!*

She remembered the comment she had made to Ms. Pratt about *The War of the Worlds*. That was a story about Martians invading Earth, trying to wipe everyone out so they could claim the planet for their own.

Louisa's imagination ran wild, and she couldn't help but wonder . . . was something like that actually happening now?

Just the thought of it made an icy chill drift up and down Louisa's spine.

CHAPTER 10

WHEN LOUISA ARRIVED at her house, it was quiet. That was to be expected—her parents were still at work, and they wouldn't be home for another couple of hours. No, the house was quiet because there was no power there, too. Even from outside, Louisa could hear the silence. No hum from the central air conditioner. In the corner of her eye she saw an old red pickup truck. But it wasn't where she expected it be. It was parked askew, halfway up her neighbor's front lawn. Crazy neighbors. Great. What was it with people in this town? When she clicked the button on the garage-door opener, nothing happened.

Sighing, she leaned her bike up against the side of the garage. She took her house key and went in through the front door. Inside, it was stifling. Gross. Hot. Sticky. Call it whatever you want, it wasn't pleasant. Louisa decided the best course of action was to go to the kitchen, get some ice packs, and place them on the backs of her knees. She read somewhere that if you cooled down your pulse points, it would cool down your entire body much faster. It was one of those life hacks. After grabbing the ice, Louisa made her way to her bedroom. She wanted to take advantage of the daylight and continue her reading. After all, if the power didn't come back on before nighttime, how would she find out all about Zarrko or the Stone Men from Saturn?

Hiking up the steps to her bedroom, Louisa kicked off her shoes at the top of the stairs. The sound startled Ash, who had been lying on the floor right outside Louisa's door. Louisa made an *Oops!* face, then bent down, rubbing her dog right on the ear the way he liked it.

"Sorry about that, Ash," she said in a soothing

voice. "You wanna come in and sit on the bed with me while I read?"

Louisa stood up and walked into the room, with Ash padding right behind. She opened the largest window. At least there might be a little breeze, even if it was hot. Then she flopped onto the bed with her book, and Ash jumped up, too. The window was right above her pillow, which she used to prop her book up as she read on her stomach. The ice packs on the backs of her knees were already working as she felt the hot breeze from the window waft over her. Then she cracked open the *Thor A to Z* book as Ash put his big, goofy head on her lap.

A fast reader, Louisa was already on the letter *J* (reading all about Jotunheim and the Frost Giants who had bedeviled Asgard for centuries). She looked up from the book at the setting sun. There was still no power.

"Really, Ash?" she said to her dog. The canine's ears perked up at the mention of his name. "What are we gonna do?"

She hadn't called the power company yet, only because she figured that if the problem affected the whole town, then they certainly already knew about it. What was her one little phone call going to do? Still, with her parents at work, and it being so quiet, Louisa felt a little spooked. And lonely.

It had been more than a week since the move, and while Louisa was pretty independent, she still didn't feel completely comfortable in the house all by herself. Louisa decided what she really needed right now was to hear her mom's reassuring voice and a terrible joke from her dad. Grabbing her cell phone, she resolved to give them a call and tell them all about the weird power outage and the freaky explosions at the library.

Pulling the cell phone out of her backpack, Louisa was surprised to see the phone was dead. There was no power. It was about as useful as a paperweight.

Freaked out, Louisa threw the phone on her bed. What was going on?

She had charged the phone overnight. It was at 100 percent battery this morning! Louisa hadn't even made one call or so much as checked her e-mail. So how could the phone be out of power already?

Unless . . .

Could the comet somehow be responsible?

"It *is War of the Worlds*," Louisa whispered.

A shudder went up her spine as she left the room, Ash trotting beside her.

Downstairs in the kitchen, Louisa decided that a snack would be just the thing to take her mind off of all the weirdness, so she went for her old standby—the peanut butter and banana sandwich. With no power, she couldn't use the toaster, but that was okay. "Not everything in life has to be toasted," her dad liked to say to her. This because for a solid year when she was five, all Louisa would eat was toast. Peanut butter toast. Jelly toast. Ham on toast. Lettuce and tomato on toast. She would actually eat almost anything . . . provided it was served to her on toast.

Louisa grabbed a paper towel and put it down on the counter. Then she reached for the big jar of peanut butter and the loaf of bread right behind the towel. She took out two pieces, and spread a generous helping of peanut butter on the bread with a knife.

"Just take a deep breath," Louisa said to herself.

Ash whined next to her, sniffing the peanut butter.

"You hungry?" Louisa asked Ash. "You want a little peanut bu—"

DING!!

Louisa practically jumped out of her skin as she heard the microwave oven come to life. She whirled around and saw the appliance on the counter, its timer counting down backward from twenty seconds.

19 . . .

18 . . .

17 . . .

What was happening? Was the power back on? Louisa glanced nervously around the kitchen. No. Nothing else was on. Not the refrigerator, not the lights, not the air-conditioning—nothing.

11 . . .

10 . . .

9 . . .

Ash started barking like a wolf, which he never did. That freaked out Louisa more than anything, so she grabbed him and ran out of the kitchen as fast as she could.

3 . . .

2 . . .

1 . . .

Louisa was already out of the house and halfway across the street with Ash when she heard the microwave explode.

CHAPTER 11

THE EXPLOSION WAS still echoing in her ears. She ran to where she had parked her bike, grabbed it, jumped on, and started to ride. Ash raced along beside her. They burned rubber down the driveway and didn't look back. The dog was long, lean, and muscular, and kept pace with the bike as Louisa made it to the end of the block. Louisa didn't let up, and neither did Ash. She pedaled and pedaled, fear giving her legs power Louisa didn't know she had.

What . . . just . . . happened? Louisa thought, completely freaked out. *First there was no power*

at all, and then, suddenly, the microwave starts up? Counting down? And explodes?!?

She wanted to call her parents and tell them what happened. They needed to know, and maybe they could help. Maybe it had something to do with the power plant? Reaching down into her pocket, she pulled out her cell phone. Her hand felt for the ON button. She pressed it.

Nothing.

The phone was still dead. She might as well have been carrying a brick, for all the good the phone was doing her now.

With her phone not working, there was no way for Louisa to contact her parents and tell them about the exploding microwave. Besides, even if she could reach her parents, how would they get to her? Would their car even work? No other cars seemed to be.

As the seconds passed into minutes, Louisa grew more and more worried. For herself, for Ash, for her parents. For the entire town. What was going on?

Her legs kept on pumping and didn't let up until

she made it to the one place where she might be able to get some help.

The library came into view, and Louisa started to feel a little less anxious. Ms. Pratt's car was still in the parking lot. Louisa thought that was a good sign. Then she remembered the power situation. Her car probably wasn't working. Maybe Ms. Pratt walked home? She didn't know where Ms. Pratt lived. Again, Louisa's heart started racing. She needed a friend right now, bad.

Louisa rolled right up to the front doors of the library on her bike, and jumped off. The bike slid over on its side, and the front tire was still spinning as Louisa burst through the library doors. Ash came right along with her, panting heavily.

"Ms. Pratt!" Louisa called out as she ran inside, looking for the librarian. "Ms. Pratt!"

"Louisa?" Ms. Pratt said, stepping out from behind the front desk. She immediately saw that Louisa was full of fear. She ran over and gave Louisa a big hug. "Are you okay? What's wrong?"

"It's literally War of the Worlds! My microwave . . .

the power . . . it's . . . there was an explosion, and . . . I can't reach my mom and dad, and . . ." The words came pouring out of Louisa now.

"Easy, take it easy," Ms. Pratt said. "Tell me what happened."

Fifteen minutes later, Louisa had finished telling her story to Ms. Pratt. Ash was happily lapping up water from a makeshift bowl (aka Ms. Pratt's lunchbox), and Louisa had calmed down a little bit.

"What do you think it is, Ms. Pratt?" Louisa asked. Maybe because she had been reading so many books about Super Heroes and Super Villains, Louisa's mind automatically raced to the culprit being some kind of super-powered menace. After all, wasn't it more exciting to think that the Green Goblin or the Leader was behind the strange power outage? Louisa ran her fingers through her now tangled hair. She took a deep breath and quickly wiped her forehead, which was just starting to produce growing beads of sweat. Louisa looked up at Ms. Pratt, sincerely. "What do you think it all means?"

As if in answer, the library doors opened again. A kid, maybe a little older than Louisa, walked right in, rubbing his shaggy black hair with one of his hands. "I'll tell you what it means," he said. "But you won't believe it."

CHAPTER 17

"KEI!"

Ms. Pratt looked excited, happy . . . almost relieved to see the boy standing in front of Louisa. The boy looked a little disheveled, rumpled, like he had been traveling for a while. And he looked tired—he had big bags under his eyes. At once, Ash started to bark. But it wasn't the bark he reserved for the usual strangers, or when someone rang the doorbell at home. It was his happy *New friend! New friend!* bark. He ran right up to the kid and jumped a little, putting his paws on the kid's chest and going in to lick his face. The kid laughed, trying to cover his face, but it was too late. The damage was done. He got a face full of dog spit.

"Down, Ash, down!" said Louisa, and the dog immediately got down on all fours and trotted back to her. "Good boy," she said.

The kid wiped the dog's greeting from his face and walked into the library. Now it was Ms. Pratt's turn. She gave him a big hug, and the kid named Kei appeared to squirm, just a little.

"You made it!" exclaimed Ms. Pratt. "I wasn't sure if you even got the message, not with the power problem, and—"

"I got it, and I'm here!" Kei said, still squirming. "Wow, your hugs are kinda tight!"

Ms. Pratt laughed, then let go. "Sorry about that. It's just been a weird day, and I'm happy to see another familiar face." The librarian suddenly realized that Louisa was still standing there, very much afraid, and said, "My manners are terrible. Louisa, this is Kei. Kei, Louisa."

Louisa cleared her throat, trying to sound as

normal as possible. "Hey, um, I'm Louisa. But you already know that. So, Kei, is it? Are you from Woodstock, too?"

Kei shook his head no. "I'm here because I'm kind of following a mystery. Ms. Pratt got in touch with me, and I think my mystery is your mystery, too."

"Oh, good," Louisa answered. "I thought you were here for the incredible scenery and the seafood."

Kei and Ms. Pratt looked at Louisa, then at each other. Then they looked back at Louisa.

"It was a joke," Louisa said. *This is going to be a long afternoon*, she thought.

"Louisa, I think you might want to join me and Kei for a . . . conversation," Ms. Pratt said. She wiped a bead of sweat from her forehead and motioned to a nearby table with three chairs. The librarian sat down, and Kei, then Louisa, followed.

"What are we talking about?" Louisa asked. "Just how freaky it is that one night a comet shows up, and the next thing, all the power in town goes off? Like, *all* the power? Even cell phones?"

Ms. Pratt nodded as Kei pulled out his cell phone. He pressed the ON button.

It worked.

"Wait!" Louisa said, practically jumping out of her chair. "Your phone! It's working! How is that possible? Nothing in this crummy town is working! There's no power!"

Kei shook his head. "The problem isn't the power," he began. "Something is jamming the power."

"Something?" Louisa asked. She felt her throat tighten a little as she spoke.

"Some. Thing," Kei replied.

"I'll get us some water," said Ms. Pratt, "while you explain."

CHAPTER 13

"**YOU SAID** some *thing*. Like a person? Who is doing this? Is it like, Martians? Or is it like, a Super Villain or something? Like Doctor Octopus? The Wizard? One of those guys?" Louisa asked. Despite being afraid, the situation was also kind of exciting. It was like reading about some sensational Super Hero fight, except it was actually happening to her!

"No, not Martians. And not a Super Villain," Kei said. "Not like a typical one, anyway."

"So who is it?" Louisa said. "*What* is it?"

Ms. Pratt returned with three bottles of water and set them on the table. Everybody took one and began to drink. Ash looked up from the floor at the people drinking. This made him realize that he had his own water, and he walked back over to the makeshift bowl for another drink.

Kei shook his head. "First thing's first. The power is being jammed. More like something has taken control of the power. And the machines."

"The machines?" Louisa gasped. "You mean, like my exploding microwave?"

"Your microwave exploded?" Kei asked, concerned.

"Her microwave exploded," Ms. Pratt said.

"You're gonna need a new microwave," Kei said, joking. No one expected a goofy comment in the middle of such a serious conversation, and everyone broke up laughing.

"Well," Louisa started, "if something's controlling the power, then how is your cell phone working? I've, uh, done a little reading about cell phones, and that doesn't seem like a standard feature."

Ms. Pratt gave Louisa a sly grin. "By 'a little reading,' Louisa means she's read enough books that she could probably build her own cell phone," Ms. Pratt said.

Kei smiled at Ms. Pratt and then looked at Louisa. "My phone has a little, uh, something that prevents it from happening."

Louisa stared at Kei. She knew that he wasn't telling her everything. She kept looking at him.

Ms. Pratt broke the silence. "You can trust her, Kei," she said. "Just like you trust me."

At last, Kei relented. "Everyone knows me as Kei, but some people also know me by another name. Kid Kaiju."

Louisa stared at Kei, saying nothing.

"And the reason why your town has no power is because of an alien."

Again, more staring.

Then Louisa leaped to her feet, practically dancing in place. "An alien? Here? In Nowheresville?" she exclaimed. She seemed genuinely excited, until she let the facade drop. Louisa frowned. "No way! This is like, the most boring place on earth! Except for the library, Ms. Pratt, which you know I love!"

Kid Kaiju took a drink of water. "Well, it's true."

Louisa started pacing, and Ash, picking up on her

vibe, started to pace right alongside her. "Do you really expect me to believe that an alien is causing a simple power outage?"

"There's nothing simple about this power outage," said Ms. Pratt. Kid Kaiju nodded in agreement.

"I . . . I . . . no, I guess there isn't," Louisa said, stumbling over her words. Both Ms. Pratt and Kid Kaiju were right. It would be one thing if the power was out and it was just the lights and electricity that weren't operating. But things with batteries— like cell phones? There was no reason they wouldn't still work.

"Look, I don't blame you for thinking this is just absolutely bonkers," Kid Kaiju said. "If I were you, I guess I'd think the same thing. But I'm telling you, it's the truth."

Louisa didn't know what to think. She was being asked to believe a person whom she had just met, who was telling her that the cause of their problem was a big, bad creature from outer space. Louisa didn't like strangers. The only reason she wasn't rolling her eyes was because he knew Ms. Pratt.

"Look, no amount of my talking is going to make you a believer," Kei said, as if reading Louisa's mind. "Maybe it's better if I show you something."

"Sh-show me something?" Louisa said, unsure.

"It's okay, Louisa," said Ms. Pratt. "You can trust Kei. I trust him."

"Allllll right, then," Louisa said. "What do you want to show me?"

CHAPTER 14

"OKAY, YOU CAN OPEN your eyes now!"
Kid Kaiju said.

A minute or so ago, he asked Louisa and Ms. Pratt
to walk with him into the library parking lot. Louisa's
first thought had been, *Is he going to show me his
car?* But then she realized that Kid Kaiju was only a
little older than she was, and there was no way that
he had a driver's license.

"'Curiouser and curiouser,'" Louisa said, quoting
Alice's Adventures in Wonderland. She felt a bit silly,
as if she were playing a game like a little kid. Still
she played along and now removed her hands from
her eyes.

What she saw from her vantage point in the parking lot was not a car.

No, it wasn't a car at all.

She didn't know *what* it was.

"This is Hi-Vo," Kid Kaiju said, pointing at a hulking, blue-and-white creature that crackled with electricity all over its body. Two bright white lights beamed where a person would have eyes. The creature even had a mouth, or what appeared to be one—it was a constantly sparking line of electricity that seemed to imitate a human smile.

"H-h-hello, Hi-Vo," Louisa stuttered, finding herself waving in spite of herself.

In response there came a series of popping sounds from Hi-Vo's "mouth." It sounded like a shower of sparks. It raised its right hand and mimicked Louisa's waving action.

"Hi-Vo is a . . . uh . . . new friend of mine," Kid Kaiju said. It was always pretty awkward explaining the presence of a huge electricity-powered creature.

Louisa couldn't believe it. She looked at Hi-Vo, standing there, right in front of her. Then she turned to Ms. Pratt. "How are you not freaking out?!?" she called to the librarian. "This . . . this is incredible!"

"I've met some of Kei's friends before," Ms. Pratt said warmly. "Not Hi-Vo, he's new. But he seems just as nice as all the others."

"He's . . . Is he an alien, too?" Louisa asked, fascinated.

"No, he's not an alien," Kid Kaiju said. "More of a . . . well, I hate to say 'monster,' but I guess you could call him that. But he's a good monster."

"A good monster," Louisa said. "That's a thing?"

At the word "good," everyone turned to hear a bark come from the library doors. Ash came running out, trotting up to Louisa, wagging his tail.

"Your dog doesn't seem to mind Hi-Vo," Kei said. As if in response, Ash looked at Hi-Vo and opened his mouth. His tongue lolled out, and he started panting.

Hi-Vo tilted his head, looking at the dog. Then he bent over, kneeling, still looking at Ash. Hi-Vo opened his mouth and imitated the panting, releasing a shower of fine sparks into the air around him. This delighted Ash, who started to run around in circles, jumping, as if trying to catch the sparks.

"He . . . he's like a child," Louisa observed.

"Kind of, yeah," said Kid Kaiju. "Hi-Vo is here to help me. Us. His powers are all electricity based. He might be the only thing that can help us stop Trull."

"Who's Trull?" Louisa asked.

The look that Kid Kaiju gave Louisa made her blood run cold.

CHAPTER 15

THE YELLOW CLOUD was growing angry and impatient.

It had spent the last few days recovering from the battle with the flying man. The one who had summoned the lightning from the sky, who had hurt it so.

It needed time. Time to regroup, to build its energy.

It had hidden in their machines.

It had been the microwave, a pathetic device. It absorbed what energy it could, and in a fit of anger

exploded. Better to destroy such a pitiful housing and move along.

Before that, it had been the red pickup truck that had driven from the outskirts of Woodstock, all the way into town, finding its way to this house. And before that, it had been the old, rusted-out dump truck that had run out of gas along the side of a lonely road.

And before that, it had been the comet that wasn't really a comet. It was a piece of debris from a flying vehicle that it had taken over. The vehicle that the flying man had destroyed, causing it to flee in the first place.

The yellow cloud seethed with an anger that only grew as it flowed through the air. It was remembering the past, and how it had come to this world in the first place.

It had been so long. So long since it had first arrived on Earth. Since it had encountered . . . what were they called? Humans? They were the bane of its existence. It had landed in a place full of dirt and humans and . . . machines. Machines that it could control. It held the humans hostage, forcing them to do its will. They would help it destroy their own planet, and aid it in its quest to leave.

Yes, the humans. They alone stood between it and its ultimate goal of destroying everything in its path, then leaving this miserable little backwater world. Yes. It wanted very much to leave for the stars, then conquer the many worlds beyond.

But it was not meant to be. The humans had thwarted it somehow. When its ship crashed on earth many years ago, its bodily form was destroyed by humans. It had been scattered to the four winds, a formless mass of yellow energy. Just waiting. Waiting for the day when it would attack anew.

The day that it had finally taken over a craft, it would have headed into space, were it not for the flying man. The flying man trapped it on this planet once again.

Its anger grew and grew.

The yellow cloud drifted from the burnt husk of the microwave oven, through the house, and out the door. It had been growing stronger since it had seized control of all the electricity in this place. It would keep growing stronger, too. It would take control.

Over everything.

The yellow cloud floated into the air, up and up. It came into contact with some power lines. And then, it seemed to melt right into those wires, as if it had never been there at all.

The power lines suddenly sizzled, and they glowed yellow.

CHAPTER 16

LOUISA'S HEAD WAS SWIMMING.
She was a fast reader and used to processing and devouring information, like it was a whole pizza and she hadn't eaten for a week. But even with that, this was an awful lot for her to take in all at once.

There was Kid Kaiju, who apparently controlled his very own monster, a friendly electrical beast named Hi-Vo. Somehow, her new friend, the librarian Ms. Pratt, knew Kid Kaiju. Heck, even Ash thought Kid Kaiju and Hi-Vo were pretty cool.

Oh, and also the power-sucking alien who threatened her new home. There was that, too.

"So what exactly is going on?" Louisa asked. "How did you just happen to show up?" she said, addressing Kei. "How do you know him, Ms. Pratt? How? What . . . ugh . . . my head!"

Ms. Pratt laughed, and sat down next to Louisa, who was now sitting on the curb outside the library. "I've known Kei for a while. Kei, maybe you want to tell Louisa about *Tales to Astonish*."

"What's *Tales to Astonish*?" Louisa inquired.

Kei quickly filled Louisa in on the amazing world of *Tales to Astonish*. A website, a forum devoted to the strange and unusual—creatures, monsters, aliens, all the out-of-the-ordinary things that adults usually dismissed as fakes, frauds, or figments of somebody's overactive imagination.

"People from all over the world use *Tales to Astonish* as a resource to find out about the hidden world all around us," Kei said. When he saw Louisa start to chuckle, Kei realized what he was saying was a little bit corny. But it was true. "It's a database of the weird. There are monsters constantly trying to take over our planet. I use *Tales to Astonish* to keep track of them. Then my monsters and I try to help stop the bad guys."

"Wait . . . you have *more* monsters?" Louisa said, incredulously. Kei nodded. "You're no joke."

"I am not. And I'm here because of that comet. I think that comet was actually an alien being named Trull. And there's only one person on Earth who knows anything about Trull. . . ." Kei said, his voice trailing off. He looked at Ms. Pratt. She smiled.

"Ms. Pratt?" Louisa asked. "How . . . aliens . . . what? Aren't you just a librarian?"

"*Just* a librarian?" said Ms. Pratt, a little offended. "There's no such thing as 'just' a librarian, Louisa. We are the guardians of all knowledge on this planet!" She laughed a little, and so did Louisa.

"My grandfather, Phillip Pratt. He encountered Trull many, many years ago. In Africa. It arrived in a comet, or something that my grandfather thought was a comet. He was there, working on an irrigation project. Something to help people, bring fresh water to help grow crops. Anyway, Trull arrived and took over the machines at the project site."

"How did it take over the machines?" Louisa asked.

"We're not sure, exactly," Ms. Pratt said. "Grandfather's notes weren't very clear on that topic. It manifested itself as some kind of glowing yellow cloud, when it wasn't taking over the machines. It actually managed to seize control of an enormous steam shovel and forced my grandfather and the other people there to build him some kind of doomsday weapon! This Trull wanted to destroy our world then head back out into space, where it would continue its path of destruction."

Louisa thought for a moment, captivated by Ms. Pratt's story. "But how did your grandfather stop Trull? I mean, we're all still here, so I assume he stopped him. Or maybe the Avengers . . . ?"

Ms. Pratt smiled at Louisa as Ash trotted over, putting his head on her lap. She patted the dog on the head. "The Avengers never even knew what was

happening. All that my grandfather's journal says is that an elephant stopped Trull that day, and the alien was never heard from again. Well, until now."

"An elephant?" Louisa said. "Really?"

"Really," Ms. Pratt replied.

"Huh. Curiouser and curiouser."

Louisa was about to ask Ms. Pratt a question when a sound cut her off.

Like a short circuit, electricity sparking, an explosion.

The power lines above the library suddenly came to life, exploding in a shower of sparks that rivaled the Fourth of July.

CHAPTER 17

THEY COVERED THEIR EYES as the sparks rained down upon them. The sparks dotted the pavement, dancing on the ground as the shower continued.

"Look out!" shouted Louisa. She scooped up Ash around his tummy and pulled the dog under her as she ducked down. Kid Kaiju and Ms. Pratt fell to the ground as well, shielding their faces from the shower of sparks.

Ash barked. Louisa replied, "Exactly! Keep your head down!"

There was a loud sound, like something snapping,

and the power lines fell to the street, a trickle of sparks flowing from their severed ends.

Then they saw it.

A yellow cloud.

It seemed to flow out of the power lines and into the air, drifting with the breeze, then not drifting. Staying in place. Then it moved slowly, as if it were looking. Looking for something.

But looking for what?

Louisa could only watch, entranced, as the yellow cloud began to move through the air once more. It hovered above her for a moment, then seemed to move with purpose toward . . .

. . . Ms. Pratt's car.

It had been parked at the library since the morning, before the power went out. And there it remained in the parking lot, an immobile object. The yellow cloud flowed through the air and was now hovering just above the car. Slowly, the cloud descended, before it seeped in through the car's hood and into the vehicle itself.

"Do you see that?" Louisa shouted. "What is that?"

She didn't have to wait long for her answer.

The sound of static erupted from the vehicle. Then came a voice, even though no one was sitting in the car: "I-AM-TRULL!"

Then the car came to life, its engine revving so hard, it sounded like a threat. It sounded like the car had been thrown into gear with the brakes on, and the tires were straining, ready to roll.

"I-AM-TRULL!" said the voice again.

Louisa wasn't sure exactly what was going on, but she knew it wasn't good. How could the car be talking? There was no one in the car.

That's right, she thought. *There is no one in the car. No one but Trull.*

The car's engine continued to roar ominously. The brakes let up, and it began to slightly edge forward. A jerk here. A jerk there. It was as if the car were alive and getting ready to pounce on prey.

Kid Kaiju grabbed Louisa by her shirt. Louisa, in

turn, grabbed Ash. Ms. Pratt was right there with them.

"I think we might need to—" Kid Kaiju started as Ms. Pratt's car screamed to life. Somehow, the vehicle reared up on its two back tires and came skidding across the parking lot, heading directly for them!

"RUN!" Kid Kaiju shouted.

CHAPTER 18

"I-AM-TRULL!"

Louisa dove out of the way of the monstrous car as it slammed down on its front tires, right in the spot where she had just been standing. A second later and Louisa would have been flatter than . . . well, she wasn't sure what she would have been flatter than, but it would be pretty flat, she knew that.

"Louisa! Over here!" The voice belonged to Ms. Pratt, who had rolled out of the way of her own killer car and into a ditch on one side of the parking lot. "Run, now!"

The car was circling back as Louisa picked herself

up off the pavement. If she ran fast enough, she might be able to make it. Her legs pumped, and Ash was right beside her every step of the way. Louisa could hear the car's engine behind her, coming closer and closer. The noises that came from beneath its hood were almost unearthly. It sounded like its engine had been pushed to its limit, like it was about to explode.

At last she jumped off the edge of the parking lot and rolled into the ditch. She landed on her right elbow and yelped in pain as she continued to roll. Coming to a rest, she looked up and saw the car jump over the spot where she, Ms. Pratt, and Ash were now lying.

The car slammed into the grass, skidded, then got up on its two rear wheels once more. It was seeming less and less like a car now, and more and more like a kind of . . . monster.

"I-AM-TRULL!" shouted the car.

"Yeah, yeah," said Louisa, out of breath. "We know!"

"Hey, Trull!"

Louisa recognized the voice. It was Kei—Kid Kaiju!

The terrible car revved its engine again, and its tires tore up the grass as the vehicle raced back toward the parking lot. Louisa and Ms. Pratt rolled out of its way, and Ash jumped, too.

Louisa looked up from the ditch to see Kid Kaiju standing in the parking lot. Behind him was Hi-Vo, who somehow appeared much taller than he had when she first met him.

How is that possible? Louisa thought. *Wait, how is any of this possible?*

"Let's see what you got, Trull!" Kid Kaiju taunted the alien.

The car roared, as if in response to Kid Kaiju's challenge. But before it could gun its engine to move forward, Hi-Vo struck. It released a blinding burst of blue-and-white energy at the car. The vehicle stopped where it stood, still propped up on its two rear wheels. The energy seemed to dance all around the car, weaving in and out of every nook and cranny.

As quickly as it had come, the energy subsided.

The car fell over, landing on its front two wheels, hard.

Louisa gasped as she saw a yellow cloud flow out from the now-motionless car.

"Trull!" shouted Kid Kaiju, pointing at the yellow cloud.

"*That's* Trull?" Louisa said in disbelief.

"That's the alien," Kid Kaiju said, watching as the yellow cloud seemed to disappear. "He manipulates electricity. He can take over machines, make them come alive, and he uses them to destroy. Everything."

CHAPTER 19

THE CAR SAT there in the library parking lot, a thin, constant stream of white smoke coming from its hood. It was clear that not only had the car seen better days, it probably wouldn't be seeing any more, either.

"I'm gonna need a new car," Ms. Pratt said, scratching her head.

Louisa started pacing the parking lot, waving her hands in the air. Ash followed her. If he had hands, he probably would have waved them, too. Instead, the dog was content to follow his friend, moving his head up and down every time she waved her hands.

The dog barked. Louisa looked down at her friend. "Exactly," she said.

Then she whirled around to look at Kei and Ms. Pratt. "This is utterly fantastic," she said, shaking her head. "My parents wanted me to go outside, see the town, make some friends. And here I am with the town librarian, a total stranger, and a total stranger's electric monster, trying to save the world from *another* monster!"

Ash barked.

"Exactly!" Louise exclaimed, answering Ash.

Not knowing what to say, Kei and Ms. Pratt stood there, silent.

"Did I miss anything?" Louisa asked, not expecting an answer.

"No. No, that about covers everything," Ms. Pratt responded. Louisa jerked her head to look at the librarian. She had to laugh.

"This seems like something out of a Roald Dahl story," Louisa said. "Like *Charlie and the Chocolate Factory*, but, y'know, weirder."

"I read that story," Kei said. "That's the one with the giant chocolate river, right? And the kid dives into the chocolate and starts drinking it but gets stuck in the pipe?"

"Really?" Louisa said, looking at Kei. "That's all you got out of that story?"

Kid Kaiju laughed. "We need to keep moving," he said. "Hi-Vo was able to disrupt Trull, to prevent him from inhabiting that car anymore. But Trull can take over anything that uses electricity. Anything. Anywhere there's a machine, you'll find Trull."

"'Anywhere there's a machine, you'll find Trull,'" Louisa echoed. "What are you, his agent?"

Kid Kaiju gave Louisa a strange look, like he didn't get what she was saying.

"Sorry," Louisa said. "Joke. My dad would have gotten it."

CRASH!

Louisa stood up abruptly as she saw something go flying through one of the library windows.

CRASH!

Another window.

CRASH!

Another.

"Our computers!" shouted Ms. Pratt. "Trull's taken control over the library's computers!"

As if on cue, the three computers that had flung themselves through the library's glass windows were now advancing on Louisa, Ms. Pratt, and Kid Kaiju.

One of the computers whipped an extension cord around Ms. Pratt's ankle, catching her by surprise.

An eerie, disembodied voice screamed from the computer, "NONE-SHALL-ESCAPE-TRULL!"

CHAPTER 20

LOUISA WASN'T SURE where the sudden burst of bravery had come from. Maybe it came from reading so many books and following the adventures of so many heroes. But it had, and so she jumped right on the computer that had grabbed Ms. Pratt's ankle. The other two computers wrapped their extension cords around Louisa's arm, trying to make her release her grip on the other computer's extension cord.

But Louisa wouldn't let go. It was like a game of tug-of-war. She had played tug-of-war with Ash since he was a puppy. Louisa would hold one end of a small rope with her hand, Ash grabbed the other in his mouth. They would pull for hours, neither one giving an inch. Sure, it got pretty slobbery.

But Louisa was good at tug-of-war.

Ash barked, seized the wild extension cords in his mouth, and started to pull. He was up for a good game of tug-of-war, too.

Giving one mighty pull, Louisa yanked the extension cord right out of the computer, freeing Ms. Pratt. Ash held the other two cords fast in his mouth, and Louisa grabbed those and yanked, too.

"Louisa! Grab Ash, move!" yelled Kid Kaiju.

She hugged her dog and rolled, as Hi-Vo blasted the computers.

The blue-and-white energy danced around the hardware as the computers somehow continued to move with a mind of their own. It was like they were still advancing on Louisa and Ms. Pratt! At last, the computers slowed down, then stopped moving altogether.

A yellow cloud appeared, drifting away from the computers.

Ms. Pratt untangled the cord that had wrapped itself around her leg. Louisa did the same with the cords on her arms.

"We're running out of time," Ms. Pratt said with urgency. "We have to find a way to defeat Trull now. He's already finding a way to resist Hi-Vo's powers."

Louisa turned and looked at Kid Kaiju. He nodded in agreement. Then she turned her attention back to Ms. Pratt. She had an awful lot to learn about librarians.

As Louisa and Ms. Pratt got to their feet, Ash started to whine. He tilted his head in that way that dogs do when they hear something high-pitched, something that people can't hear.

"What is it, Ash?" Louisa asked, rubbing the dog's back. "What do you hear?"

And then she heard it, too. A high-pitched whining sound. Almost like a teakettle. But stronger.

It was coming from inside the library.

And it sounded like it was getting closer.

Closer.

Louisa's ears were assaulted by the piercing whine of the library's boiler as it crashed through the wall of the library.

CHAPTER 21

LOUISA HAD NEVER seen a boiler come to life before and try to attack anybody. In fact, most people had never seen anything like it. One thing was for sure—Louisa didn't like it. She thought that Alice must have felt a little like this when she fell down the rabbit hole. Disoriented.

Scared.

"Get out of here, you two—now!" The voice belonged to Ms. Pratt. She shoved Louisa toward Kid Kaiju. He grabbed Louisa's hand and pulled her along. Ash stuck right by Louisa, never leaving her side.

"We're not going to leave you!" Louisa yelled.

"What she said!" Kid Kaiju added. "We're all monster hunters here, right? We stick together, right?"

The boiler screeched and belched hot steam into the air. There was an awful clank of metal on metal, and then the now-familiar voice: "I-AM-TRULL!"

"Go now!" Ms. Pratt shouted again. "I can take care of myself. You two leave, fast as you can! I'll follow!"

Louisa couldn't just leave her friend. She had already left behind her friends in her old home. She wasn't about to leave a new friend.

The boiler was now walking, and coming closer and closer. Ms. Pratt turned her back to the kids, facing Trull.

"If we don't split up now, then Trull might catch us all!" Ms. Pratt said, placing herself between the kids and the alien invader. "Splitting up is the only chance we have of stopping it!"

"Ms. Pratt, no—" Louisa protested.

"No, she's right!" Kid Kaiju said, pulling Louisa. "We need to get out of here while we can!"

As Trull made its fury known with a great gush of steam, Louisa grabbed her bicycle and hopped on.

"Get on!" she yelled, and Kid Kaiju hopped on behind her, holding on to her belt.

They were off as Louisa pedaled furiously.

"What about Hi-Vo?" she called out.

Kid Kaiju responded, "Don't worry about him! Just pedal!"

And pedal she did, pumping and pumping.

They didn't even look back as they heard the boiler explode.

CHAPTER 22

LOUISA LITERALLY had no idea how long she had been riding her bike with Kid Kaiju holding on to her. A half hour? More? Less? Her nerves were a wreck. What she wouldn't give to be curled up at home with her copy of *Thor A to Z* right about now. She bet there was something pretty interesting about Hela she could learn. She was kind of like the Sandman, and had fought Thor a bunch of times. Hela ha—

"LOUISA!"

It was Kid Kaiju. Louisa realized she must have been lost in her own thoughts, pedaling on auto pilot. How long had Kid Kaiju been calling her name?

"Sorry, I wasn't here, I was . . ." Her voice trailed off.

"It's okay, I think we're far enough away," Kid Kaiju said. "Stop up there."

"Up there" was a park on the outskirts of town and just at the edge of the massive nature reserve. They had ridden Louisa's bike as far north as they could go and didn't stop until there were mountains and trees as far as the eye could see.

And no power lines.

No cars.

An old streetlight, but it was broken. Glass shattered, no bulb.

Which meant no Trull.

"We can take a break for a minute," Kid Kaiju said, hopping off of Louisa's bike. "Catch our breaths."

"Catch 'our' breaths?" Louisa said as she got off her bike. She promptly rolled over onto the grass. Ash was immediately by her side, licking her face. "What do you mean 'our' breaths? I've been doing all the pedaling!"

Kid Kaiju laughed. "True, true." He sat down in the grass next to her.

"I feel terrible," Louisa said. "I know it was the right thing to do, leaving Ms. Pratt. But we have to go back. We have to try and help her."

"We can't do that, Louisa," Kid Kaiju replied. "Ms. Pratt was right. We have to find a way to stop Trull ourselves, and trust that Ms. Pratt can take care of herself."

Louisa sat up for a minute, and Ash followed her. "But how? I mean, how do you stop something like Trull? He doesn't even have a body. He's just a big yellow cloud that can take over machines. Even Hi-Vo couldn't . . ." Louisa looked around, realizing something was missing. "Where is Hi-Vo, anyway?"

"He's around," Kid Kaiju said mysteriously. "He'll be here when we need him."

"I just don't see what we can do," Louisa finished. "I wish I was reading this in a book so I could skip ahead and see how the story ends."

"You do that, too?" Kid Kaiju asked. "Skip ahead to see how the story ends?"

Louisa started to laugh. "Oh yeah! I mean, not all the time. But some times, sure! I can't wait. And it doesn't spoil the book for me. It's not the destination, it's the journey."

Kid Kaiju nodded.

In all of this, Louisa realized something—how much she missed her parents. Most kids she knew were always talking about what a pain their mom and dad were, how they wouldn't let them do what they wanted—have a phone, have fun. But not Louisa. She loved her parents. What she wouldn't give to have them with her right now.

Suddenly, there was a loud CRACK!

And the streetlight exploded in a shower of sparks. The wires from inside the post began to whirl around like whips. Then there was the terrible voice.

"KNEEL-BEFORE-TRULL!"

CHAPTER 23

HOW DID TRULL FIND US? Louisa wondered. There were no power lines, no cars, nothing mechanical for miles. The only thing around was a broken, rusty old streetlamp that hadn't seen use in who knew how many years.

"It must be that light," said Kid Kaiju, as if reading Louisa's mind. "Even though it was broken, there must have been an active current in there somewhere."

The streetlamp—Trull—wrenched itself from the ground with a screeching, metallic sound. The wires whirled around it, whipping the air, slicing, coming closer and closer to Kid Kaiju and Louisa.

"Any ideas?" Louisa said, as the Trull-light closed in on them. Ash barked at the light, growling from the corners of his mouth.

"I-WILL-DESTROY-YOU!" croaked a menacing, tinny voice that came from the streetlight.

"Not the idea I wanted to hear," Louisa replied as she and Kid Kaiju took several big steps backward. The Trull-light continued forward, its wires whipping and snapping at the ground, sparks now showering from their ends.

But Ash didn't budge. The dog held its ground, growling.

"Ash!" Louisa called. "Get over here! Now!"

The Trull-light cracked one of its wires, aiming for Ash. At the last second, the dog jumped, running over to Louisa.

"Come on, come on, come on . . ." muttered Kid Kaiju.

What is he muttering to himself about? Louisa thought. *What is he waiting for?*

A moment later, Louisa had her answer. She felt her hair stand on end—like static electricity?

And just like that, he was there. Hi-Vo. Standing with Louisa, Kid Kaiju, and Ash, and towering above them. He had to be at least ten feet tall! But where had he come from?

Hi-Vo cocked his head as he looked at the Trull-light. His eyes crackled bright and white, and grew bigger, as if really giving his opponent a look. Then Hi-Vo gave a shrug of his great, big blue shoulders, and unleashed a powerful blast at the alien menace.

ZZZZZZRRRRRAAAAKKKK!

The Trull-light lost control of all the whipping wires, and they flung themselves around and around the post. Blue energy cascaded around the post, rendering the Trull-light immobile.

"That's gonna slow him down," Kid Kaiju said, "but it's not gonna stop him. Ms. Pratt was right. Trull is somehow finding a way to resist Hi-Vo's powers!"

Hi-Vo seemed to hear what Kid Kaiju was saying. He looked at Kid Kaiju, squinting at his much smaller friend. The hisses and pops of static that came from his mouth . . . well, if Louisa didn't know better, she could have sworn it was a sigh.

The Trull-light seemed to be frozen in place for the moment. But unlike before, with the computers and the car, there were still signs of life within the lamp. The wires writhed on the ground.

"We need to get out of here, right now," Louisa said. She hopped back on the bike, motioning for Kid Kaiju. He jumped on as Ash started to run at a full gallop. Then Hi-Vo blasted the Trull-light once more for good luck.

As Louisa pedaled her bike, she looked up and around. And she saw them.

Streetlights.

All old, and broken, and useless.

And Trull could take over any of them at any moment.

CHAPTER 24

"WHERE ARE WE GONNA GO? Everything is mechanical!" Louisa shouted. "And where did Hi-Vo go? How does he change size like that?"

Louisa was pedaling the bike so fast that Kid Kaiju was actually having trouble just hanging on, let alone trying to carry on a conversation and explain something as complicated as Hi-Vo.

"It's complicated," said Kid Kaiju. "Hi-Vo, I mean. I'll explain when we have a little more time."

Louisa nodded. Her head kept bobbing up and down, as she looked from the road up to the streetlights and back. Searching, looking for any sign of Trull coming to attack them. Nothing yet. So far, so good.

"We can't go through town," Kid Kaiju said. "Too many cars. Each one of those things would be a weapon for Trull. He'd smash us in a hot second."

Louisa thought for a minute. A blur up above caught her eye. Was it a spark? In one of the dead streetlights? She couldn't tell. Maybe it was just her nerves.

Yes, just nerves, she thought. *Please let it be just nerves.*

Ash barked as he ran slightly ahead of the bike. *The poor dog must be ready to collapse,* Louisa thought, *and he just keeps on going. He's gonna get the biggest dinner ever after this. If we live that long.*

"Wait a minute!" Louisa said, her voice shattering the silence. Kid Kaiju practically slid off the back of the bike. An idea started to burn bright inside Louisa's brain as she remembered something she had read recently. "You said Trull consumes electricity—right?"

"Um, well, yeah. Basically. That's what it seems like, anyway. I mean, that's what it said on *Tales to Astonish*, and that's what Ms. Pratt said that her grandfather—"

"Great! So why not give Trull all the electricity he wants—and then some?"

Kid Kaiju was quiet for a moment. "Like . . . give him an overload?"

"Exactly!" Louisa gushed. "Give him so much electricity that his body can't handle it. He'll short out! At least, that's what I read."

"Yeah, it's possible. I mean, that could work. But where are we gonna get enough power to do that?"

"Power is not a problem," Louisa said, smiling for the first time since Trull began his attack. "My parents work for a company called Win-X! It's a renewable power plant—wind power! If we can lure Trull to the power plant, we might be able to destroy him!"

Louisa grew more excited as the plan came together.

"That's a pretty big 'if,'" Kid Kaiju shot back. "It

might work . . . or it might make Trull so powerful that he destroys the planet!"

"What do you mean?" Louisa asked, looking nervously at the streetlights up above.

"Ms. Pratt said something about it. Something she found in her grandfather's journal. No one knows what Trull's limits are, or if he even has any limits. We could destroy Trull, or turn him into a supercharged power battery."

The blue creature was gone. The smaller ones, the humans and their four-legged companion had also fled. Now it was just Trull.

Trapped.

At last, the blue energy that had rendered it nearly inert dissipated. Once more, Trull freed itself from the mechanical husk that it called home, and a cloud of yellow energy floated into the air.

And then, Trull thought. The light. It had worked before. There were many such broken lights ahead. It could easily transfer from one to the other. In no time, it would be upon those miserable humans and that blue energy beast. Trull would attack and add the blue beast's powers to his own.

And Trull would be truly invincible. This pitiful planet would fall before his unlimited might. Then Trull would leave this devastated world behind and seek his destiny among the stars. For there were other planets to conquer, more power for Trull to absorb.

And Trull would start by seizing and laying waste to this tiny town.

CHAPTER 25

"**HOW ARE WE** gonna get Trull to follow us all the way out to the power plant?" Kid Kaiju asked Louisa. She had a plan. Louisa was sure that her plan would work. Now all she had to do was convince Kid Kaiju.

The kids and Ash were now in familiar territory. Well, familiar to Louisa, anyway. They had made their way from the remote park back to Louisa's neighborhood, taking back roads and avoiding the machine-filled streets.

Still, there were the streetlights. And now that they were "back in civilization," the power lines.

But in a way, that was exactly what Louisa wanted.

"I'm working on that," Louisa said as she steered her bike toward her house. "The power plant where my parents work is in the middle of nowhere. I mean, *really* in the middle of nowhere. It's about a half hour west of town, and there are no streetlights, no power lines, no nothing. There's no way for Trull to follow . . . unless . . ."

Louisa's voice was cut off by a sudden skidding sound. She had clutched the hand brakes on her bicycle hard, coming to a sudden stop right in front of her house. Ash barked, happy to be home, and ran up to the front door, panting.

"Unless what?" Kid Kaiju said. "You can't leave me hanging like that."

"Where's Hi-Vo?" Louisa asked, looking around. "We're gonna need him if my plan has any chance of working."

Kid Kaiju jumped off the back of Louisa's bike, and he took a few steps back. He held up something that resembled a double-A battery. He pressed the top of the "battery," a small, raised bump. As he did so, a streak of blue light erupted from it. And quick as you please, there stood Hi-Vo! Except he wasn't ten feet tall this time. He appeared to be a little taller than the size of an average person.

"Okay, how did you do that?" Louisa asked.

Hi-Vo's eyes grew big and white, and he waved at Louisa. The thin white line that stood in for his mouth curled up at the ends. Was that a smile?

"He definitely likes you," Kid Kaiju said. "Hi-Vo can change his size at will. He can also transform himself into pure energy. I can carry him around in these," he said, pointing to the "battery" that he held in his right hand. "Just a push of the button, and Hi-Vo comes out to play."

"Huh. That is just about the coolest thing ever," Louisa said, amazed. "Well, let's get to work!"

"This is never going to work."

The voice belonged to Kid Kaiju.

"What do you mean?"

That was Louisa.

"All Hi-Vo has to do is jump-start my parents' old car and get it running! I've seen him do all kinds of incredible things today. Are you telling me that he can't start a car?" Louisa said, nudging Kid Kaiju.

Ash was there, too. The dog looked at Kid Kaiju, hung his mouth open, and panted, his tongue hanging out.

"It might. I mean, we'll try it, sure. I guess the car is probably the quickest way for us to get to the power plant, but . . ."

"But what?" Louisa asked. She turned her head to see Hi-Vo standing next to her parents' old car, regarding it as a child looks at something it's never seen before. He reached out to touch it with an electric-blue finger. There was a sizzling sound as Hi-Vo's finger connected with the car. This seemed to please Hi-Vo, who made that funny smile of his.

"I don't know how to drive a car, okay?" Kid Kaiju said, a little exasperated. "I don't know how to drive a car. And even if I did, I don't have a driver's license. Do you? Know how to drive a car? Or have a driver's license?"

"Um . . . well, I . . ." Louisa stammered. The answer to both questions was a very obvious no. She was only ten!

"Yeah, I didn't think so," Kid Kaiju said. "But we don't have a lot of options. Hi-Vo, do your stuff, man. Can you get this car started?"

And with that, Hi-Vo bopped the hood of the car with a big, blue fist, and the hood opened. Hi-Vo moved back just a little, and again, the thin white line that was his smile played across his face.

Hi-Vo reached a blue hand under the hood, and a moment later, the engine hummed to life.

CHAPTER 26

"**I'D LIKE TO GO** on the record as saying this is a really awful idea," said Kid Kaiju, his eyes hidden by his hands.

"Oh, stop!" said Louisa, who was sitting behind the wheel of her parents' old car, backing slowly out of the driveway and into the street. Kid Kaiju sat in the passenger's seat next to her, and Ash was in the backseat. Hi-Vo had gone back into his little battery home.

"Everybody buckled in tight?" Louisa asked. She checked her seat belt, then looked back at Ash. Her parents had installed a doggie seat belt in the car just for him. He was all buckled up and lying down

on the backseat. Then she turned toward Kid Kaiju. He was also buckled up, and still looking at the road through spaces between the fingers that covered his eyes.

"Come on, how hard can it be?" Louisa put the car into drive and hit the gas pedal.

The car lurched forward, and Louisa quickly slammed on the brakes.

"Can we go back to the driveway?" Kid Kaiju said.

"Why?" Louisa asked.

"To get my stomach."

They had been on the street in front of Louisa's house for about ten minutes. Louisa figured that it was time well spent practicing how to drive before Trull showed up. She actually got the hang of the automatic transmission pretty fast. She had gone from herky-jerky newbie to legit kind-of-OKAY driver. Even Kid Kaiju was impressed. Enough that he wasn't looking at the world through splayed hands any more.

As they began to make their way to the power plant, the sun was just starting to set on the horizon.

"You're sure you know where you're going?" Kid Kaiju asked, looking down the tree-lined road before them.

Louisa nodded. "Sure, I—of course I know where I'm going," she answered. "Why wouldn't I know where I'm going?"

"Well, you didn't know how to drive, either," Kid Kaiju jabbed.

"And yet here we are," Louisa chuckled.

Without warning, there was an explosion. Everyone's head turned. Louisa hit the brakes.

The explosion hadn't come from inside the car. No, it was outside. But where? Louisa looked around, and then she saw it.

A streetlight. The bulb had blown out, and sparks rained down on the sidewalk below.

"Trull," Louisa said.

She gunned the engine and sped off down the road. Behind her, streetlight after streetlight became brilliantly illuminated, then exploded. The explosions chased after Louisa and her friends.

◦ ◦ ◦

At last, Louisa, Kid Kaiju, and Ash had left the more populated part of Louisa's town and moved out to the highway. No more power lines or lights. Just them, and one car right behind them.

Wait.

What?

Louisa did a quick check in her rearview mirror. Sure enough, another car had come out of nowhere and was now following them. It was a bright-red, brand-new sports car, a little too flashy for a small town like Woodstock. But with Trull sucking all the power from the town, how was the car running? Unless . . .

"NO-ONE-ESCAPES-TRULL!"

The voice was coming from the car behind Louisa.

CHAPTER 27

FOR SOMEBODY WHO had just learned how to drive a car, Louisa was doing an impressive job of keeping one step ahead of Trull.

The alien-possessed car was relentless in its pursuit, swerving with Louisa every time she swerved. Still, she kept the pedal to the metal, and the kids were making a beeline for the power plant.

"How did you learn to drive so fast?" Kid Kaiju said.

"Where else do kids learn how to drive?" she answered without skipping a beat.

"Video games?" Kei asked.

Louisa kept her eyes on the road and shook her head. "My parents!"

WHAM!

The Trull-possessed car slammed into the kids' car, and everyone inside lurched forward.

"IT-IS-USELESS-TO-RESIST!" came the Trull voice through the air.

"Do you think Hi-Vo might be able to lend us a hand?" Louisa asked.

"I was just thinking the same thing," Kid Kaiju said. He produced the "battery" from his pocket and pressed the button. A moment later, Hi-Vo materialized on the hood of their car. His sudden arrival startled Louisa, who swerved into the left-hand lane, then back into the right.

"Whoa!" she hollered. "Good thing there's no one else on the road!"

Hi-Vo scrambled to the top of Louisa's car, unleashing flashing bursts of brilliant blue-and-white light at the Trull-possessed car behind them. Some blasts missed, while others connected.

"Any luck?" Louisa asked, as she kept on driving, eyes on the road in front of her.

Kid Kaiju turned around, and saw Ash with his head plastered to the seat. When he looked through the rear window, he saw the Trull-possessed car was still coming. Hi-Vo hit the alien right in the grill with concentrated energy bursts, but it didn't seem to even slow Trull down.

"Nothing," said Kid Kaiju, dejected. "Hi-Vo's blasts don't seem to have any kind of effect any more."

"He's distracting Trull, though," said Louisa, looking for a silver lining somewhere in this black cloud. "That's something. Hopefully it'll be enough to get us to the power plant."

A short while later, the kids were very nearly at the power plant. Trull had kept pace every step of the way. Hi-Vo was able to keep the alien at bay, but Trull seemed almost unstoppable.

The first thing Louisa saw as they pulled up to the power plant were the endless rows of giant windmills. They stretched off to the horizon. Each had to be at least a few hundred feet tall. Every one of them had multiple enormous blades. They weren't working yet, of course.

Louisa hoped they would be working soon enough. For all their sakes.

"Hold on!" she shouted as she made a hard right turn off the highway toward the entrance to the power plant. The wheels of the car squealed, and dirt kicked up behind them. She floored the gas, and the car took off down the side road for the power plant. The entrance way was lined with dead high-powered floodlights, which were useless in helping Louisa keep to the road. Luckily, she had her headlights.

The Trull-possessed car pursued.

A few minutes later, Louisa pulled into a dirt parking area. She hit the brakes then unbuckled herself. She looked out the window and saw the Trull-possessed car rapidly closing in on them.

"Move it!" Kid Kaiju shouted. Without a word,

Louisa threw open the rear passenger door, opened Ash's buckle, and grabbed her friend.

They dove out of the way just as the Trull-possessed car collided into theirs.

CHAPTER 28

"I HAVE HAD ENOUGH explosions for one day," Louisa said as she watched her parents' old car go up in flames. "Seriously."

"Agreed," Kid Kaiju replied, picking himself up off the ground.

The Trull-possessed car was on fire too, having smashed into Louisa's vehicle. Smoke billowed upward into the sky, and Louisa was certain she saw a hint of yellow mixed in.

Trull.

Where was he headed to now? Louisa looked around at the power plant. Make that the lack-of-power plant, because as expected, nothing was working. Trull had seen to that already. The giant floodlights that dominated the parking lot were all out.

"The floodlights . . ." Louisa said softly, almost to herself. "RUN!"

Louisa tugged on Kid Kaiju's jacket, pulling him away from the parking lot. As soon as there was movement, Ash was off like a shot, running right along beside them.

And just like that, the floodlights came to life.

Then exploded, one by one.

"THERE-IS-NO-ESCAPE-FROM-TRULL!"

Sparks and broken glass cascaded down on the parking lot as Louisa, Kid Kaiju, and Ash moved. Up ahead, Louisa spotted one lone building. That had to be the control center, where her parents would be working. If they could just make it there, they might be able to catch their breaths while they figured out how to put their plan to stop Trull into action.

As the lights continued to burst behind them, Louisa wondered: With the car explosions and now the lights, why hadn't her parents come running out to see what had happened? She thought the worst. . . .

Suddenly Louisa spotted a small building. it was the control center! The door to the control center wasn't locked, so Louisa flung it open, and she, Kid Kaiju, and Ash ran inside. They didn't bother locking the door or finding some way to block it—with Trull's powers, none of that would be able to keep it out.

"We're inside," said Kid Kaiju. "Now what?"

"Now we find my parents. The plant is still in its testing phase, but they'll know how it works. Do you think Hi-Vo will be able to give the windmills a jump start, like he did with the car?" Louisa asked, hopeful.

"If anyone can do it, it's Hi-Vo!"

They ran down a short darkened hallway. A couple of windows there let in a little of the dying light from outside, which helped. At last, they made it to a door marked CONTROL ROOM. Louisa opened the door and gasped, "Mom! Dad! We need your help!"

She stood, frozen in her tracks, unable to say another word.

Louisa's mom and dad were there, but they couldn't answer. They were laid out on the floor, unconscious.

A control panel in the room sparked and glowed an eerie yellow, which dominated the room.

"THEY-BELONG-TO-TRULL-NOW. . . ."

CHAPTER 29

"**WHAT HAVE YOU** done to my parents?!?" Louisa shouted, balling up her fists, ready for a fight. She couldn't believe this was her. In just a few days, she had gone from a shy kid who preferred to keep her head buried in a book to a world-saving alien hunter, ready to squash a bad guy if they so much as harmed a hair on her parents' heads. They were her world.

There was a pause, then a burst of static from the control panel. Then, the horrible, detached, tinny voice spoke. "THEY-ARE-UNHARMED. THEY-WILL-HELP-TRULL."

More static.

"YOU-WILL-HELP-TRULL. THE-BLUE-ONE. THE-ONE-WHO-HURT-TRULL. GIVE-HIM-TO-US. WE-WILL-TAKE-HIS-POWER-AS-OUR-OWN!"

The voice cut out once more.

"He wants Hi-Vo," Kid Kaiju said, stating the obvious.

Ash turned his head and whined, then trotted over to Louisa's mom and dad. He started to lick them both on their faces.

"What are we gonna do?" Louisa asked Kid Kaiju. "We have to get my mom and dad out of here. Then we have to get this plant started up so we can—"

Before she could finish her sentence, there was a loud banging sound.

"What was that?" Kid Kaiju said.

Louisa jumped back as all the lights inside the control room came on at once, and the hum of electricity dominated her ears.

"POWER."

Trull's voice, followed by the crackling of static.

Louisa had hoped that Hi-Vo would be able to turn the power plant back on and get the wind turbines moving. But now, Trull had done it. It must have sensed the potential for power this place had. Louisa had an idea.

"We have to get out of here!" she said urgently. "Hi-Vo is nothing compared to this power plant! If Trull absorbs the electricity generated by these windmills, it might become so powerful that nothing can stop it!"

Kid Kaiju looked at Louisa, not getting it. Was she telling Trull what to do? Then Louisa raised an eyebrow, and he got it. It wasn't a warning for Trull. It was her trying to goad Trull on.

"YES!-MORE-POWER-FOR-TRULL!"

It was taking the bait.

"WE-WILL-CONSUME-ALL-THE-POWER-FROM-THIS-PLACE. AND-FROM-THE-BLUE-ONE. GIVE-HIM-TO-US-NOW!"

The room began to crackle with electricity. Through a window, Louisa could see the windmills beginning to slowly turn, generating electricity.

Then she saw something else through the window.

Lights. Lots of them. They were a ways off, but they seemed to be coming closer.

She squinted and realized what they were.

Headlights.

The high-pitched whining of tortured, overworked car engines soon filled the air, as Kid Kaiju and Louisa dragged her parents out of the control room.

Electricity arced from the control panel, narrowly missing Louisa as she pulled her mom from the room. Kid Kaiju followed close behind with her dad. Hisses and pops exploded from the control room now.

Trull was getting angry.

"THE-BLUE-ONE! GIVE-HIM-TO-US!"

They were in the hallway now, and the lights began to flicker on and off, faster and faster.

"Hurry!" Louisa shouted as she dragged her unconscious mom toward the door.

"We need Hi-Vo!" Kid Kaiju replied, pulling Louisa's dad.

"You can't! That's just giving Trull what he wants!" Louisa said, worried for Hi-Vo. She had known him only a short time, but she had grown attached to the childlike monster.

"He can take care of himself!" Kid Kaiju shot back as they threw open the front door of the small building and made their way outside into the dark.

Hitting the button on the "battery," Kid Kaiju stood back as Hi-Vo suddenly appeared in his ten-foot form.

It was good timing, too. Because a circle of cars was now driving around the control center, lights flashing on and off, on and off, engines revving. Behind them, the control center lights flickered.

It was do or die.

CHAPTER 30

THE CARS CIRCLED, faster and faster. They were drawing nearer. The lights continued to flash on and off. It was dizzying, disorienting.

"GIVE-US-THE-BLUE-ONE!" came Trull's voice, from all the cars at once.

Hi-Vo opened his white electric mouth, and a hiss of static issued forth. He was angry! Louisa had never seen Hi-Vo angry. The creature's white eyes narrowed, and he hunched over, motioning for both kids to get behind him. They did, and then Hi-Vo extended his arms outward, turning his hands so the palms faced out.

Then he attacked.

Intense waves of blue-white light erupted from Hi-Vo's hands. It was blinding, and both Kid Kaiju and Louisa had to turn away. They huddled around Louisa's parents, protecting them. Ash barked as he stood side by side with Hi-Vo.

For a brief moment, Hi-Vo looked at the dog and the dog at Hi-Vo. They seemed to know they were on the same side.

The cars continued to circle, but were now stopping and starting, stopping and starting. It was Hi-Vo's blasts that were doing it. Trull's power was being stretched too thin among all of the cars. While Hi-Vo still had the power to disrupt Trull from taking over machines, the power was growing less and less. Trull was getting used to it and was now desperate to add the monster's powers to its own.

"IT-IS-USELESS-TO-RESIST-TRULL. GIVE-US-YOUR-POWER. NOW!"

Without another word or another sound, one of the cars was on its rear wheels and hurtling toward the control center!

In a blur, Hi-Vo grew another ten feet and scooped

up Louisa, Kid Kaiju, and her parents in his enormous blue hands. The monster took a huge step out of the way as the car came crashing into the control center right where they had been standing.

The car exploded, and Hi-Vo's body shielded his human friends from the worst of it.

"Way to go, Hi-Vo!" Louisa shouted.

As the control center went up in flames, the windmills behind them began to turn faster and faster. They appeared to be out of control now. That meant they would be generating more and more electricity, more than they were built to produce. There would be an overload . . . an overload that Trull would be only too eager to consume.

Now all that remained was for Louisa to figure out how to get Trull to follow them up to the windmills. She turned to look at Hi-Vo. Hi-Vo looked at her and smiled with his funny, electric mouth. They stayed that way for a moment. Louisa couldn't believe what it was like, having a giant monster as a friend. She felt like Max in Where the Wild Things Are.

"Are you thinking what I'm thinking?" she said to Hi-Vo.

The creature tilted his head slightly. Then he nodded.

And then Hi-Vo ran right for the circling cars.

Right into Trull's death trap.

"HI-VO! NO!" Kid Kaiju yelled, calling for his friend to come back. But it was too late. Hi-Vo was already running right for the Trull-controlled cars.

"He—he knows what he's doing," Louisa said, placing a hand on Kid Kaiju's shoulder. "He's buying us time. Distracting Trull so we can lure him to the windmills!"

"I know you're right," Kid Kaiju said. He looked at Louisa and for the first time she saw fear in his eyes. "But, what if Trull absorbs Hi-Vo's powers? What if Trull absorbs . . . all of him?"

"It's just like Ms. Pratt," Louisa said, gently reminding Kid Kaiju. "Remember? She distracted Trull so we had a chance to get away and fight. Now Hi-Vo's doing the same thing. We have to trust him. We might be the only thing keeping Trull from taking over the world."

Louisa was right, and Kid Kaiju realized it. "Then let's get going."

They dragged Louisa's parents off to the side, under a small group of trees. "Ash," Louisa said, pointing at her dog, "stay." The dog dutifully sat between Louisa's parents. He would guard them with his life.

As Louisa and Kid Kaiju ran toward the windmills, they saw Hi-Vo blasting at the circling cars. One by one, Trull was flinging the cars at Hi-Vo, and one by one, the creature deflected them with his incredible energy powers. Was it Louisa's imagination, or did Hi-Vo seem smaller now than he had just a moment ago? Was he losing power?

They had to act fast.

"Trull!" Louisa hollered as loud as she could. "Do what you want to us! But stay away from the windmills! They're generating too much power! We'll all be killed!"

The remaining cars suddenly screeched to a halt. It was so abrupt, in fact, that Hi-Vo actually did a double take.

There was a strange sound that began welling up all around the power plant, growing louder by the second. It was like a mix of static and a sick coughing. A moment later, Louisa realized what it was.

It was the sound of Trull. Laughing.

"THAT-IS-A-FITTING-WAY-FOR-YOU-TO-DIE . . . AND-FOR-TRULL-TO-BECOME-INVINCIBLE!"

The laughing continued. It was a nauseating sound, and Louisa wished it would stop.

"TRULL-WILL-DESTROY-THIS-WORLD, THIS-WORLD-THAT-HAS-CAUSED-HIM-SO-MUCH-PAIN. THEN-TRULL-WILL-LEAVE, TO-CONQUER-THE-STARS!"

There was more laughing, and while Trull was entranced with his new master plan, Hi-Vo took the opportunity to grab two cars and smash them together. Now there was only one left.

One car, whose engine revved unexpectedly, as the car roared away at top speed.

Heading right for Louisa and Kid Kaiju.

CHAPTER
32

~~KID KAIJU AND LOUISA~~ were stuck in the middle, halfway between the Trull-possessed car and the windmills. The windmills weren't moving, of course. But the Trull-possessed car was. And fast. It was rapidly closing the distance between them.

"This is not a good plan!" Kid Kaiju yelled. He was used to being in the thick of things, fighting alongside his monsters, the Avengers, you name it. But now it was just him, Louisa, and a killer car.

"It's the only plan we have!" Louisa fired back as they sprinted toward the windmills. The Trull-possessed car was sparking electricity all over as it

practically flew along the ground, heading right for them and the windmills.

Every footstep carried Louisa and Kid Kaiju closer to the windmills.

Every footstep brought Trull closer.

And closer.

Louisa swore she could feel the hot sparks coming from Trull fall against her neck.

"NOW!" Louisa shouted.

CHAPTER 33

IT HAPPENED SO FAST, and yet, to Louisa, it all seemed to happen in slow motion. It was as if time had expanded, each minute, each second dragged out to hours. Like H. G. Wells's time traveler in *The Time Machine*, Louisa felt like she sat outside of time, recording everything as it occurred:

Trull, right behind them.

The windmills, right in front of them.

Trull, screaming, out of control, hungry for power.

The windmills, spinning faster and faster. So fast, Louisa thought they might fly away.

Diving out of the way of the car. Kid Kaiju to the right, Louisa to the left.

The car, colliding into the first windmill.

The sound of metal on metal. Wrenching, twisting, screeching.

An explosion.

Being thrown backward, rolling down a hill.

Looking up from the ground, watching.

The fireball.

Bright. Brilliant. Orange. Red. Yellow.

Electricity, arcing all around.

A scream.

Louisa? Kid Kaiju? Mom and Dad?

No.

Trull.

Trull was screaming.

"NOOOOOOOOOOOOOOOOOOOO!!!!"

The scream was truly horrifying. Trull, taking on all the power the windmills were generating. Too much power. More than Trull could possibly contain. The electricity continued to arc from the windmills to the car.

Louisa saw a yellow cloud rising from the car, as if trying to escape the arcs of electricity. But it couldn't. It was trapped inside an electric prison.

Trull was trapped.

"IT-CANNOT-END-LIKE-THIS!"

More screaming. The electric light show grew even brighter, and Louisa and Kid Kaiju both had to shield their eyes.

"TRULL-MUST-ESCAPE! THE-STARS-BELONG-TO-TRULL!"

But despite all his protests, despite how he resisted, Trull could not escape. The being of living electricity was close to its end.

The windmills whirled, faster and faster. More electricity. The yellow cloud, pulsing now, somehow growing less and less.

And then, another explosion. The biggest one of all.

Louisa and Kid Kaiju hugged the ground. Beneath her she felt the earth shake and shimmy, almost like an earthquake. A few hundred yards behind them were Louisa's parents, safe with Ash. Looking up, Louisa saw fire in the sky as the windmills shorted out, one by one. The electricity had stopped arcing. The car was a blackened husk.

And Trull?

Louisa saw a yellow cloud, or what was left of it. It could no longer hold itself together. The last bits of Trull drew apart from each other and blew away into the night air.

CHAPTER 34

"**LOUISA!** My Lord, are you all right?!?"

The voice belonged to Louisa's mom. She and her dad were running across the ground toward the spot where Louisa and Kid Kaiju lay on the ground.

They were all right! Louisa thought. The last explosion must have woken them up. Louisa picked herself up off the ground, dirty, rumpled, and glad to be alive. She ran over to her parents and gave them each a huge hug. They stayed that way for what seemed like forever. Louisa didn't want to let them go ever again.

"What—what happened here?" Mr. Brooks said,

looking at the fire and the ruined windmills and the burned-out control center behind them. "The last thing I remember, we were running a test on the windmills, when there was a power surge. Then . . . then I can't remember anything."

"Me either," said Mrs. Brooks. "What are you doing here, Louisa? You could have been hurt! Or worse!"

"It's a long story, Mom," Louisa said. "Um, by the way, this is Kei. He's my friend. He, uh, helped me pull you guys out of the control center before it burned down."

"You're a hero, then," said Mr. Brooks as he took Kei's hand and shook it.

"Yeah, I guess," said Kid Kaiju. "That's me!"

Louisa's parents had invited Kei to come back to their house and call his parents, but Kei had begged off. He said that he had his own ride, and Louisa smiled at that. She knew exactly who the ride was—Hi-Vo.

Before they left the power plant, Kei gave Louisa his cell number. She knew they would stay in touch.

As she looked at the note that he wrote, Louisa saw something scribbled beneath the cell number:

"Talestoastonish.com. Sign up. Post. I'll see you there!"

Louisa smiled.

It had taken a while, waiting for a cab to pick them up at the power plant. The ride back home seemed to take forever, but Louisa was happy just to have her parents safe. Ash was pretty happy about it, too. He sat in the backseat, stretched out across everyone's laps, relishing in all the scratches and pets and attention.

When the cab pulled up at the Brookses' house, Louisa was surprised to see someone standing on the front porch, waiting.

"Who is that?" Mrs. Brooks asked.

Louisa flung the door open, and she ran toward the porch, Ash following.

"Ms. Pratt!" Louisa cried out, running right into the librarian's arms. They hugged, and Ash jumped up on the librarian, giving her a big lick on her cheek.

"How was your night?" Ms. Pratt asked.

"Oh, you know," Louisa said nonchalantly. "Maybe I'll write a book about it!"

CHAPTER 35

THE NEXT MORNING, Ms. Pratt casually walked by Louisa who was sitting at one of the brand-new library computers. An anonymous donation had been made to the Woodstock Public Library and, from the look on Ms. Pratt's face when she opened the check, it seemed like it had been more than enough to cover the damage.

Ms. Pratt quietly set down a bowl of apple slices. The apple was completely peeled. Just like Louisa liked it.

"Thanks, Ms. Pratt! I was wasting away over here." Louisa said with a smile.

"Oh, any time," the librarian responded. "Heard anything from Kei?"

Louisa turned the computer screen so Ms. Pratt could see that Kid Kaiju had just responded to a message Louisa had sent him on *Tales to Astonish*.

KidKaiju:
Glad to hear Ash is still a complete doofus. Will you ask him if he misses me? You can send me his response in dog language and I will try to translate. Dang, I need to find myself a good sidekick. Maybe I'll draw one tonight.

Oh! And before I forget, send me those books you recommended. They sounded really good!

Okay. Now off to Avengers Tower . . . just kidding. Or am I??

EPILOGUE

A FEW DAYS LATER, and the power plant was still a smoldering ruin. Workers had arrived to seal it off, to make sure all the power was shut off properly and there was no danger. So much damage had been sustained during the battle with Trull—or the "power surge," which was what everyone except Louisa, Kid Kaiju, and Ms. Pratt believed it to be—that it would take weeks, months, to restore the plant to operational status.

"This place gives me the creeps," said one of the workers as he pulled a big roll of wire-mesh fencing from one post to another. They were erecting a fence around the perimeter to make sure nobody got too close to the site and injured themselves.

"Ahh, it's your imagination," said another worker. She went to the truck they rode in on, opened the door, and pulled out a boom box. "How about some tunes? Take your mind off of how creepy this place is."

The other worker shrugged his shoulders as the boom box blared out a tune.

They went back to rolling out the fence, and putting it into place.

"Ooooooh baby, baby . . ." came the song from the boom box.

"Ugh," said the creeped-out worker. "I hate this song."

Suddenly, there was the sound of static crunching. It came from the boom box.

"Hey!" said the worker who had turned on the boom box. "Stop messing with my tunes!"

"I didn't touch your tunes!" yelled the creeped-out worker.

The other worker walked over to the boom box. The static was really loud now. She turned the dial on the boom box, trying to get another station. All she got was static.

"Huh," she said, scratching her head. "It must be broken."

As the workers turned back to their fence, the sound of the static waned and was replaced by a tiny, wavering noise.

"Trulltrulltrulltrulltrulltrulltrulltrull . . ."

THE END?

MARVEL

MONSTERS UNLEASHED!

BUNN • McNIVEN • LEISTEN • CURIEL

MONSTERS
UNLEASHED!

WHEN GIANT MONSTERS KNOWN AS LEVIATHONS START RAINING FROM THE SKY AND WREAKING HAVOC ALL OVER THE WORLD, IT IS UP TO THE HEROES OF EARTH TO STOP THEM. BUT EVEN WORKING TOGETHER, THE AVENGERS, CHAMPIONS, X-MEN, GUARDIANS OF THE GALAXY, AND INHUMANS MIGHT BE UP AGAINST A THREAT TOO LARGE TO TACKLE. WAVE AFTER WAVE OF LEVIATHONS ATTACK, INTENT ON RAZING THE WORLD, AND IT SEEMS ONLY A MIRACLE CAN SAVE EARTH NOW...

MEANWHILE, ELSA BLOODSTONE TRACKS DOWN A PROPHECY ABOUT THE APOCALYPSE--AN APOCALYPSE THAT INVOLVES GIANT MONSTERS AND A "KING" TO RULE THEM. AND IN MISSOURI, A YOUNG BOY NAMED KEI KAWADE HAS A MYSTERIOUS CONNECTION TO THESE EPIC EVENTS...

CULLEN BUNN -- *WRITER*

GREG LAND -- *PENCILER*

JAY LEISTEN -- *INKER*

DAVID CURIEL -- *COLOR ARTIST*

VC's TRAVIS LANHAM -- *LETTERER*

GREG LAND WITH JAY LEISTEN AND FRANK D'ARMATA -- *COVER ART*

ARTHUR ADAMS WITH PETER STEIGERWALD; KIA ASAMIYA; GREG LAND; FRANCESCO FRANCAVILLA -- *VARIANTS*

JEFFREY VEREGGE -- *HIP-HOP VARIANT*

JEE-HYUNG LEE -- *MARVEL FUTURE FIGHT VARIANT*

JACK KIRBY, MIKE ROYER & PAUL MOUNTS WITH JOE FRONTIRRE
-- *KIRBY 100TH ANNIVERSARY VARIANT*

CHRISTINA HARRINGTON -- *ASSISTANT EDITOR*   **MARK PANICCIA** -- *EDITOR*

AXEL ALONSO
EDITOR IN CHIEF

JOE QUESADA
CHIEF CREATIVE OFFICER

DAN BUCKLEY
PUBLISHER

ALAN FINE
EXECUTIVE PRODUCER

AVENGERS-- FOCUS YOUR ATTACKS ON THE CREATURES ON THE *RIGHT*.

WE CHAMPIONS'LL TAKE THE ONES ON THE *LEFT*.

CAPTAIN AMERICA.

HULK.

HOPE EVERYONE HAD A GOOD BREAKFAST.

IT'S *SMASHING* TIME.

MS. MARVEL.

OR... NOT?

THE SECOND GROUP OF MONSTERS...

...THEY'RE *IGNORING* US!